WHAT YOU
DON'T KNOW
Can
HURT YOU

Glen Collins

authorHOUSE®

AuthorHouse™
1663 Liberty Drive, Suite 200
Bloomington, IN 47403
www.authorhouse.com
Phone: 1-800-839-8640

First published by AuthorHouse   3/6/2009

ISBN: 978-1-4389-6141-5 (sc)

Printed in the United States of America
Bloomington, Indiana

This book is printed on acid-free paper.

Acknowledgments

I wish I could take total credit for this enormous undertaking, but in honesty, I cannot. The completion of this novel is due only to the grace, kindness, and inspiration of God. A portion of His kindness was manifested in the support from a number of phenomenal people who He placed in my life to see me through this process. There were many times along the way when giving up would have been easy and sensible, but then God would prompt one of these beautiful people to say just what I needed to hear to keep going.

Roy W., thank you for being my sounding board when the story was just beginning to come together. *Ian Michaels "Mike M.",* one of the most creative people I know, your courage in risking it all to make your dreams come true inspired me so much to make this book happen. Then, when I was about to put it on a shelf to sit, you woke me from discouragement to a state of excitement. Thanks for being a real friend and inspiration. *Macky,* a true friend through the years, thanks for loving me unconditionally and making sure I always know it. *Ah'Lee,* a man who will try anything and usually succeed, you know I'll always acknowledge that the influence you had on my life helped make me whoever I am today. *Jock,* thank you for your critique. Your insight made me a better writer and this project a better novel. You are a special person to me. *Kevin W.*, you are truly one of the most genuine friends (and people) in the world. Your encouragement, kindness, and promotion of my talent changed the way I see my gift. *Jason,* thank you for just being there and being you. You are indeed my brother and I love you very much. *Leconiá,* my son, thanks for loving me with the same amount of fervor you use to drive me crazy. *"T²",* my biggest fan in everything I do, I don't tell you enough how much I appreciate you and your friendship. *Pastor Will and The Power Center family,* thank you for spiritually covering me, and for sincerely encouraging artistic Christians to pursue the dreams God placed in them without judgment or condemnation. *Pastor Will,* you are more than my spiritual leader, you are my mentor, confidant, and friend. *Cecil "ShaKil",* you have been a friend for longer than many of the readers of this book have been alive. You are one of the most brilliant people I know. Thank you for your insightful suggestions on this project. To my proofreader, website designer, and unofficial critic, *Tarren,* on many days you were more excited about this project than I was. Your enthusiasm often woke my creativity and shooed writer's block away. Thank you for the many late night line-by-line reviews. You are a truly talented and creative person with a phenomenal future. *Chase,* a "Johnny-come-lately" to this project, sometimes you say simple things that cause me to focus and see that this novel reaches those whose lives it is meant to change. I look forward to enjoying your intelligence, wisdom, and fun-loving spirit for a very long time.

Lenny, Victor, and Bob, thank you for sharing your creativity, vision, and style with us. Although the time was short, the world is a much better place for many people because you were here. I will ever love and never forget you.

Prologue

"This time I'm gonna fire his ass! That damn Robert Sharpe done went to sleep out there in that goddamn truck and missed punching back in from break again," Wiley snapped.

Wiley Tatum, or Tater Tatum as he was called at the casket factory, was the model stereotype of a redneck in 1960's small town Mississippi. Wiley was the foreman at the morbid factory and to look at him, you'd swear he was the ku klux klan's grand wizard. With his overtly pink face, belly hanging beyond his waist, slow southern drawl accent, and tobacco brown teeth, Tater was every civil rights advocate's image of "the enemy". On the contrary, Tater Tatum was always fair to his ninety-five percent black force of casket makers. More times than he cared to remember, Tater had bought groceries to feed the too many children of some of the struggling employees of the factory. Tater made sure that the few white men who worked at the factory worked every bit as hard as the black men and were paid the same, if not less. The men began calling Wiley "Tater" when a new toy made out of a plastic potato with removable eyes, ears, nose, and mouth became the latest kid's fad. Ironically, the toy looked just like a brown version of Wiley; and his last name being Tatum didn't help.

"I mean it this time, when he comes marching back in here talking 'bout he done overslept, I'm gonna tell his ass to walk right back out the door and go home. Matter of fact, I ain't waitin'. I know he's out there in that damn truck," Tater proclaimed, making a production of stomping across the sawdust floor.

Everyone knew Tater was going to cuss and fuss and give Robert the ever famous "one last chance" as he had given all of them at least ten times before, so no one panicked.

Tater found the ragged orange and white Chevy with the rusty muffler easily in the rock-covered parking lot and walked right up to it. As sure as he had imagined it, there was Robert sitting on the driver's side with his head laid back against the back window. Robert had pulled his "Jack's Fishing Gear" baseball cap down over his eyes and his mouth was open wide enough to fit a baseball in it.

"Robert! Robert wake yo lazy ass up! Robert!" Tater banged on the window.

Robert didn't budge. Tater snatched the door of the truck open. Robert's heavy body fell out of the truck and onto Tater. Tater ended up pinned to the ground by the literal "dead weight" of Robert's still warm and musty soulless body.

Chapter 1

"Lord Miss Letha, yo grandchillen is just as fine as dey can be! And dey so smart, just smart as rip. You ain't never gonna have no trouble outta dem."

Reverend Mullin always made a big deal over Miss Letha and her grandchildren as they filed out of Mt. Hope Baptist Church in Woolfe, Mississippi each first and third Sunday. Church services were only held on first and third Sunday's since Reverend Mullin served as the pastor for another church in the neighboring small town of Evansville which held its services on second and forth Sundays. The churches in the area would alternate on fifth Sundays hosting an area "Fifth Sunday Sang" where the entire combined congregations would sway back and forth harmonizing melodious hymns and spirituals until all hearts were overwhelmed with a sense of closeness to God and each other. Although it was the 1970's and times were changing, the pace of change was snail slow in small Mississippi towns like Woolfe. It was more like the 1950's. Modern day living as seen on television was like science fiction to the inhabitants of this area.

Reverend Mullin's special attention to the children was not as much sincere as politically motivated. Miss Letha's influence over the members of the congregation and community was powerful. Miss Letha's great grandfather was the freed slave who had been given the land from his former owner for the white rickety church that also served as the colored school for the area for many years until the new brick edifice that now stands was built. However, the accolades were appropriate. Miss Letha's grandchildren, Robert Jr., Esther, Sarah, and Calvin, were well-behaved, neat, intelligent children. Miss Letha would have it no other way. She wouldn't dare have her reputation among the people of the small communities around Woolfe blemished by the likes of her son's kids.

Miss Letha reluctantly took guardianship of the four orphans after the sudden death of their father, her son, Robert Sr. Robert was discovered in his truck by his foreman at the casket manufacturing company where he had worked since he was a teenager. An hour after he was due to return from his lunch break, the foreman decided to check if Robert had taken a nap in his truck as he often did and slept past his lunch time. When he opened the driver door of the truck, Robert fell to the ground apparently dead of a heart attack.

Robert's wife, Lizzie, remarried a younger man in Roe Creek who refused to have another man's children raised in his house, even if the other man was dead. Miss Letha was backed into a corner to do the right thing or have the community know she turned her back on her own blood. The fact that the children were "high yella" like their mother helped Miss Letha tolerate and eventually find affection for them.

Miss Letha was every black woman's voice of wisdom and instruction in lady-like manners. She was the Mother of the church and therefore she deemed it her duty to sew and bring to church a number of lace edged lap cloths to pass out to the younger ladies whose skirts were too short. Miss Letha was the one to tell the young wives, "I think you have one in the oven, Sugar," officially confirming any suspicion of pregnancy. And if a young woman was found to be pregnant out of wedlock, Miss Letha was the one to go to them and order a public apology before the entire congregation. Many pastors came and went from Mt. Hope, but Miss Letha's reign as the true leader of the people saw no end while she lived.

Chapter 2

Lizzie was the daughter of a fly by night Mulatto musician from New Orleans and an ever too gullible young country girl. However regretful the circumstances surrounding their one night of passion and untamed lust might have been, its product, Lizzie, grew up to be one of the most beautiful women of the day. It's no wonder the new colored elementary school principal in Roe Creek was dazzled by her beauty and married her six months after Robert Sr.'s death.

Of Lizzie's four children with Robert Sharpe Sr., Calvin, her youngest, inherited all of her looks and none of his father's. Lizzie's attraction to Robert Sr. was never because of his face. Many a night, she thanked God she didn't have to look at this ugly man while he made love to her. Rather, she'd close her eyes and gain her pleasure from feeling his tight muscles, wrapping her arms around his small waist, and running her hands along his ripped six pack as he trust eleven full inches inside her with synchronized rhythm.

Robert Jr., Esther, and Sarah had Lizzie's complexion but looked every bit their father's children. This was not the case with Calvin. He had his mother's beautiful hazel eyes, full lips, and wavy brown hair; a perfect face wrapped in perfect, unblemished skin. To crown this Adonis, he had his father's V cut body, which was naturally toned and showed signs of muscle before he was even fully a teenager.

However, Calvin's attractiveness came at a price. The boys in school mocked him incessantly, labeling him a "half-breed pretty boy". The constant teasing diminished Calvin's self esteem. He eventually came to loathe his light toned skin and wavy hair. He secretly longed to be as dark as the night like Gran's photos of his father, the man of whom he had no memory.

The worse torment of Calvin's life came when he and his sister, Sarah, were forced to spend a month with his estranged mother and her husband, Vernon, in Roe Creek. Robert Jr. had joined the Army and was traveling the world; and Esther was studying at Jackson State to be a teacher. Calvin had just turned fourteen and was more gorgeous than a twenty-one year old model. His body somehow had defied the years and was, at this tender age, almost fully developed.

"You think you're too good to do any work around this house don't you Yellow?" Vernon would ask. "Miss Letha has you ruined cause she's one of them color struck Negro women. Well I ain't."

Vernon seemed to resent Calvin's looks although he was the spitting image of the woman Vernon sought out, courted, and married *because* of her looks. Since it was summer and Vernon was a principal at the local black elementary school, he was home every day with the two teenagers while Lizzie worked unreasonable hours at the Wade County Nursing Home.

Sarah quickly took to the elderly Mrs. Nezzie who lived down the road. She began visiting her daily, learning her recipes for the best cakes and pies in the county. It also gave Sarah a reason to leave the house she so vehemently hated. This left Calvin and Vernon home together for the greater portion of the day until Lizzie came home shortly before dusk each day. Calvin would often look up from reading one of his many nonfiction books to find Vernon staring at him with a look of contempt on his face. Calvin did not retaliate or hate Vernon for his actions. On the contrary, he understood Vernon's apparent disgust. After all, Calvin resented his own looks more than Vernon ever could.

One night during their last few days in Roe Creek, Sarah asked Lizzie for permission to spend the night at Mrs. Nezzie's to help her bake cakes for the upcoming Annual Revival Meeting at the church. That same night, Lizzie was scheduled to work the overnight shift at the nursing home.

Later when Calvin emerged from the hallway bathroom still half wet from his bath before bed, Vernon was passing on his way to bed.

"You just like a girl, sitting in that tub all night. I ain't having no sissies staying in my house, you hear me?"

"Yessir."

That night, Calvin was just about asleep when he heard the knob turn and a splinter of light enter his room. As he turned over in the bed, he saw the silhouette of Vernon standing over him. The sight was frightening. Was he dreaming? Were his eyes deceiving him? Was Vernon really there, and why was he naked?

"You want to be a girl? You determined to have folks laughing at me for having a boy that's prettier than any girl in town aren't you? Open your mouth and see what fast girls like to do since you want to be one."

Calvin lay stunned, confused, and frightened looking at his stepfather's nude body as his eyes adjusted to the darkness. He now could see clearly that Vernon's man muscle was erect, curving upward just over his head. In the seconds that followed, a thousand thoughts ran through Calvin's mind. Among these thoughts, the most prevalent was, "what did I do to make him think I want to be a girl?"

"You hear me? Open up your mouth and suck this dick before I have to tell Lizzie how you been prancing around here half naked trying to flirt with your own mama's husband, just like you a little whore or something! You think I don't see you walking back and forth in front of me tryin' to show me how pretty you are? Now open your damn mouth and suck my dick you little yellow sissy!"

Calvin's young eyes welled with tears as he weighed the consequences of his mother thinking he was a sissy; and how much worse it would be if she told his grandmother. He slowly and reluctantly gripped his tongue between his lips and lightly licked the rock hard stem of Vernon's curved penis, a penis that wasn't quite as big as his own, and he was only fourteen. He continued this abominable oral action as Vernon stroked himself and twisted his own nipple until he came, dropping his liquid sin on his pubescent victim's face. Calvin cried silently as the hot evil cum dripped on him and the man he knew he could never speak to again trembled and grunted in sinful delight.

"Clean yourself up. And if I hear anything about this, I'm gonna whip your ass and then tell your mama how you tricked me into doing it. You hear me?"

"Yessir," said Calvin as he exerted all his effort not to burst into hiccup sobs.

Calvin kept his word and did not tell anyone what he had done for his stepfather. However, he did tell Gran that he never wanted to see Lizzie or her husband again. Gran did not ask him why, but rather slapped him hard on the face quoting, "Thou shalt honor thy mother and father boy! That's right in the BIBLE!"

Chapter 3

Calvin was always younger than the other students in his grade. He had been advanced directly from second to forth grade at Mt. Hope Elementary School because of his unprecedented aptitude. So when Calvin returned to school that faithful Fall of 1979, he entered tenth grade and therefore closed the chapter of his life labeled Mt. Hope Middle School and faced the yet to be written pages of the chapter, Woolfe High School, a defining period in his life. This transition was a very stressful one. Calvin's summer experience had been comprised of spending time with his mother for the first time since he was an infant, and being sexually abused by his stepfather. Now, he was not at all looking forward to another year of antagonizing bullies at school. Most concerning to Calvin was the fact that Woolfe High would be his first real interaction with white people.

Woolfe was the County Seat for Willard County, Mississippi and therefore was the location of the only high school in the county. Caravans of yellow buses paraded through the one-lane, paved streets of town tediously making their way to the red brick building like ants marching toward a scrap of food. Small white trailers that were used as additional classrooms surrounded the school. These trailers were needed after desegregation laws forced the formerly white school to accommodate the scores of black children formerly schooled at church schools in the rural county.

Sarah, now in her junior year, looked after her younger, more introverted brother. She was determined to make sure Calvin did not have to suffer the torments he endured in middle school from bullies. She often encouraged him to be more outgoing like she was.

"You're old enough to have a girlfriend now. The other guys are going to think you're 'funny' if you don't start acting like you're interested in girls," she would tell him. Calvin understood that Sarah was sincerely trying to help him and therefore he did not take offense at the question of his manhood, as he would have had either of his other siblings made this same statement.

Calvin's lack of self-esteem, inexperience with girls, and general self-hatred paralyzed him when it came to talking to any girls other than his sisters. A great change began when Zelda Knowles asked him to help her with her geometry homework one day.

Zelda was everything Calvin wasn't. She was confident, outgoing, and without a doubt the most popular black girl at Woolfe High. Zelda's personality was equally matched by her good looks. Her skin was the color and smooth texture of creamy peanut butter. Her silky, coal black hair seemed to always be freshly permed. Zelda definitely had it going on. Zelda was being reared by her father, Gilbert Knowles, who was a good man and a member of the Deacon Board at Mt. Hope. Her mother, Lelia, had died when Zelda was only nine years old.

Calvin eventually made it a steady habit of riding the bus home with Zelda on Tuesdays and Thursdays to help her with homework in various subjects. They would study until her father would get off work at nine o'clock and drive Calvin home to Miss Letha's house. There was never any worry from Mr. Knowles about leaving his only daughter alone with Calvin because Calvin was, after all, Miss Letha's grandson. He knew that Miss Letha would never raise a young man to be disrespectful or indecent.

"Calvin, you know my daddy says yo daddy and him was friends when they was in school. He said you don't look nothing like him though." Zelda once told him during one of their study sessions.

"I know I don't look like him. I look like my mother, but I don't want to. I hate looking like her." Calvin always found himself able to say things to Zelda that he could never say to anyone else. Their study sessions proved just as psychologically therapeutic for Calvin as they were academically beneficial for Zelda.

"Why you say that Calvin? You just about the most handsome boy I ever seen. You know, sometimes I wonder what it would be like if you kissed me with them big ole pretty lips."

Calvin's face turned the color of fresh cherries, giving away his flattered embarrassment. Again, his light complexion had betrayed him. If he were his father's color, he never would have to worry about his emotions causing his skin color to change, making him hate his paleness all the more. His eyes immediately found his feet, not knowing what to do, what to say, or where to look.

Zelda, being the take charge person she was, cupped his chin in both her hands and slowly lifted his face. She gently pulled his jawbone forward and extended her face into his and gave him, at age 14, his first real kiss.

The kiss with Zelda jumpstarted the long overdue repair of Calvin's confidence and self esteem. Eventually, it became clear to him that he was smarter than most, if not all, of his classmates. It dawned on him that his ability to reason was more advanced than that of his peers. Most of all, he realized he was not unattractive. He began to understand that, on the contrary, the attributes he previously hated were very much envied by most black boys his age, especially his flawlessly mature body. With his advanced maturity of mind, he realized that envy was the fuel that kept the bullies diligently on his case in his prior years. His understanding of these things was owed in great part to Zelda's constant boosting his confidence and ego.

In time, the last half hour of every study session was spent kissing Zelda, perfecting his technique with each experience.

When Woolfe Public Library had it's annual Damaged Books Sale, Calvin was excited to buy several books for Zelda, hoping this would encourage her to take reading and education more seriously. Calvin was falling for Zelda but could not imagine being with someone who did not fully value knowledge.

"Calvin, what in the world am I supposed to do with all these books? They not even interesting; like this one, 'English to Swahili Translations'. What do I need that for?" Zelda laughed as she questioned Calvin.

"You never know when you gonna need a Swahili word. O.k., that one may be a stretch, but I thought it was interesting. I bet you one day you gonna be glad you have that book. Wait and see. It only cost a quarter," Calvin replied.

One Tuesday evening during their study time, Zelda asked, "Have you ever done it?"

"Done what?" Calvin asked totally oblivious to what Zelda meant.

"You know, 'it'. You ever got some pussy?" She responded.

Calvin panicked. "Of course I have," lying.

"I ain't never done it. Will you do it to me?" Zelda asked.

Calvin was surprised. He assumed a girl as popular and outgoing as Zelda would have experienced everything. Following his surprise, the panic and fear returned with greater ferocity. Now he'd have to either turn Zelda down or risk her finding out he had no clue what to do.

Calvin being the quick thinker responded, "Zelda, if you've never done it, you should wait 'til you do it with your husband."

"Calvin, I thought you was gonna be my husband one day," Zelda replied, again practically knocking Calvin off his feet.

Calvin was so totally overwhelmed with love for Zelda at that moment that he wanted to do anything she asked of him. He successfully fought with all his strength to keep the tear in the corner of his eye from falling. Calvin hated that he was more sensitive than most of the guys he knew.

"My daddy won't be home from work for another hour." Zelda knew this was the perfect night.

"Alright," Calvin replied reluctantly.

He began to kiss her in the way he had instinctively taught himself, using not only his lips but tongue as well. As they kissed, Zelda began to fondle him and he felt his manhood begin to rise. Zelda unzipped his jeans and released the man-sized penis attached to the now fifteen-year-old body. She took a quick breath of shock at its size. Calvin's penis throbbed as it became harder and harder. This was the first time anyone other than he had touched his penis since he was a baby and it was blowing his mind. Zelda then removed her own blouse, unhooked her bra, and gave Calvin his first viewing of the opposite sex. Calvin gently caressed Zelda's nipples causing her to whimper in pleasure as her nipples stiffened.

This first experience was awkward and clumsy, which was normal for two virgins. Calvin came as Zelda stroked him, before he could even enter her and reciprocate the pleasure. But with practice and time, the couple found their grove and over a period of two months had sex at least ten times.

* * *

By that Spring of 1980, just before the end of the school year, the thrill appeared to be gone for Zelda and it was breaking Calvin's heart. The one person who made him feel that his life had value had become a stranger to him.

It happened suddenly and seemingly for no reason. One Tuesday, Zelda found Calvin at his locker between classes and told him she wouldn't be able to study that night because she had something else to do. When Calvin asked what it was, she snapped, "Calvin, I get tired of seeing you every *damn* Tuesday and Thursday. Sometimes I just want to do something else, ok?"

Calvin's eyes widened at Zelda's use of the word, "damn". She never used profanity with him before. His heart sank. That was the last time they ever spoke of studying or being together again.

Chapter 4

That summer, Calvin's heart ached as it never had before. The hurt he endured when he was tormented by his classmates, the hurt he felt when Gran berated him, nor even the hurt he felt when he was molested by Vernon, could compare to the agony of the overwhelming disappointment, pain, and longing he felt for Zelda.

When he could take it no longer, Calvin decided to make one more attempt to talk to Zelda and ask her how she could so easily dismiss him. He dialed the number several times, hanging up before the first ring most times; not getting an answer the other times. When he placed the call on a particular sweltering June morning, his heart pounded almost through his chest with every ring. Then just as he assumed he'd get no answer again, Zelda's father's voice came through the receiver.

"Mr. Gilbert? This is Calvin, I was wondering..."

"Calvin, Zelda isn't here. She won't be here. She's gone to Atlanta for the summer and first part of the school year, maybe the whole year." Mr. Knowles made this monumental announcement as nonchalantly as if he was reporting his prediction for next week's weather.

"But Mr. Gilbert, *Atlanta?*" Calvin was incredulous.

"Yes, son. She's spending some time over there with her aunt. Every since her mama went to Heaven, it's just been me and her and she needs to be around some women to teach her things I can't. Plus, I been a little selfish not making her spend time with her mama's folks sometime," Gilbert Knowles explained.

"Listen son, I ain't crazy. I know what you and Zelda was up to, and I know what you calling 'round here for now. You can just go on and find you another one of them girls for that. The kitchen is closed over here." At that, Mr. Knowles hung up the phone; not really slamming it on the receiver, but just a decisive, deliberate end to the conversation. As if to say, "that's that."

Calvin seemed to be able to actually hear his own heartbeat drumming in his ears. For the next few moments everything was surreal. Zelda, gone for almost a year? It was hard enough seeing her and not talking to her or kissing her, or making love to her. But not seeing her at all their whole junior year could not be real.

The possibility of Zelda staying in Atlanta for the next school year, their junior year, did become a reality. Moreover, she did not return to Woolfe until the middle of their *senior* year. Then, apparently because of the transferring back and forth, Zelda was put back a grade and would not graduate with Calvin as planned. However, it didn't matter because by this time Zelda acted as if nothing had ever happened between her and Calvin. Atlanta had changed Zelda, she was much more grown up and seemed out of place with the other students there at Woolfe High School. Calvin too, had learned at an early age what "moving on" meant. But he knew he'd always have a special place in his heart for Zelda. For some reason, he felt they had a connection that would be there forever, no matter how Zelda pretended not to notice him.

Chapter 5

High school senior year: arguably one of the happiest, most memorable years of any person's life. For Calvin, this year was a road of many winding turns, heading straight for a tragic collision.

After Zelda left, Calvin began to withdraw within himself, feeling that there was no one left to really understand him. By this time Sarah had graduated and started school in the Delta so Calvin was not only alone at school, he was alone at home. As Miss Letha grew older, her ideas of what was "proper" grew more and more outdated and Calvin was the focus of her restrictive attention. Calvin was not allowed to listen to "the devil's music", referring to anything other than gospel music. He could not attend any of the parties his friends threw. And heaven forbid he drink anything stronger than a soda. He imagined that Gran would have died a thousand deaths if she knew the things he and Zelda had done on those Tuesday and Thursday evenings last year.

By the time Calvin was a senior at Woolfe High, his oldest sister, Esther, was a senior at Jackson State and had begun dating. One Saturday afternoon, she brought home her boyfriend, Randolph, for Miss Letha to meet. Now, for any of the Sharpe children to bring home anyone for "Gran" to meet, it must be serious, very serious.

Randolph was six-foot-two, dark chocolate, muscular, with perfect white teeth. He had a low, neat haircut, not the all too common 'fro or the latest fad, the jehri curl that Gran detested so. He wasn't quite the kind of gorgeous that Calvin was, but he had a very masculine, grown up sex appeal that was undeniable. Randolph was obviously very intelligent and articulate. Miss Letha was immediately in love with his personality and the prospect of his becoming her grandson-in-law; and she made it known.

"Esther, I hope you have the good sense to keep this man. You don't run across smart, good lookin' Negroes everyday girl," Gran blurted out right in front of Randolph.

Miss Letha could barely contain her excitement at the thought of the other ladies at Mt. Hope meeting her potential new grandson-in-law. She thrived on the acceptance, reverence, and envy of others. In all her years, she never learned to enjoy life for herself; rather, she lived to impress others.

"Randolph, why don't you and Esther spend the night so you can go to church in the morning with 'ole Granny if you ain't too shame of me. Esther can make up the old girls' room for herself and you can sleep in there with Calvin." Gran had a way of making "suggestions" that were always understood to be unquestionable instructions.

Calvin choked on his piece of Gran's peach pie when she made this suggestion. He couldn't imagine sleeping in the room with anyone other than Robert Jr. Now, it was a done deal. Gran had made the call; again, with no concern for how it affected him. He did not want to think he hated Gran, because he knew it would be wrong, so he quickly put the thought out of his head.

That night Randolph slept like a baby in his mother's lap. He slept in Robert Jr.'s too small bunk bed; the bed that Calvin had dismantled and placed beside his instead of on top the same day Robert Jr. left for boot camp. The room was really too small for both beds so they appeared more like one king sized bed with a small split down the middle.

As Randolph slept like a log, Calvin tossed and turned the en
night in his own bed. Something about having Randolph lyii
there within arm's length of him bothered him and ruined his hop.
of a restful night. He couldn't for the life of him figure out why he
was so bothered. Not the kind of 'bothered' that made him angry.
It was rather the kind that possessed his thoughts so much that
every time he thought he might drift off to sleep the knowledge of
Randolph's presence shook him back to full consciousness.

That Sunday morning, Randolph woke very early after his night
of seemingly undisturbed rest.

"Morning Calvin," Randolph said sitting up in bed wrapped in
covers waist down. "I thought you country people got up before
the crack of dawn."

"We usually do, but man it's not even six o'clock yet. Gran's
not getting up for about an hour to make you guys a big country
breakfast. Sunday School doesn't start 'til nine–thirty," Calvin
answered.

"What do you mean, 'you guys'? I'm sure that the breakfast
is more for you than us. You know Miss Letha would climb Mt.
Everest for you. I can tell already you're her favorite. You should
have heard all the things she was telling me yesterday about your
academic accomplishments at Woolfe High School," Randolph
informed.

"Yeah, I'm sure." Calvin rolled his eyes with much attitude; he
wasn't surprised. Miss Letha was great at telling everyone what a
good job she had done raising her fatherless, pitiful grandchildren
and how she alone was responsible for Calvin's good grades and
academic awards.

"Sounds like *somebody* has some grandmother issues. What's
going on man? Talk to me." Randolph seemed genuinely interested,
his thick eyebrows furrowing over his brown gleaming eyes.

Although Randolph's presence in the room had made Calvin
uncomfortable all night, he strangely felt very comfortable and a
strong urge to open up to him now.

...visible to Gran. We don't talk, she just preaches ...she is consumed with what people think about her. ...ppy about my grades and awards because people pat her ...ck for doing such a good job with the fatherless burdens ...d to raise. She can hardly wait until I go to Morehouse next ...ar so she can brag about it to everyone. She's already telling Reverend Mullin that I'm going to the same school Martin Luther King went to. She's a trip man," Calvin said, sighing deeply.

Randolph thought a quick moment before speaking, the mark of a truly smart man. That small action impressed Calvin more than Randolph would ever know. "Don't feel that way man. You've got to realize your grandmother is from a totally different era than we are. She didn't have the opportunity to show how smart she was. All black women had pretty much the same future around here. The really successful ones could possibly become teachers or nurses. The others were left to pray for a good husband. And a good husband meant one who would work hard enough to feed the children and who would be too tired to hit his wife when he got home. I get the feeling your grandmother just enjoys knowing that somehow her life did produce some accomplishments, even if those accomplishments are through her grandchildren."

"Whatever man, you don't know her like I do. It's crazy around here and I don't have nobody. You just don't know," Calvin snapped back all too quickly, quicker than he could stop the words.

Calvin found himself wailing up with tears, embarrassed at his confession of loneliness. Again he hated himself for being such a sissy when it came to crying. He turned on his stomach and buried his face in the pillow determined to keep it there until Randolph either dressed and left the room or went back to sleep.

His mind raced in fear and embarrassment with wild thoughts. *How could he ever look at Randolph again after crying in front of him? What if Randolph told Esther? What if Esther then told Gran?! Why did he start talking to this nosey guy anyway?*

Then suddenly Calvin felt warm, strong fingers on his shou
pulling him away from the refuge of his pillow. He looked up
the dim light of dawn and there was Randolph, shirtless and in hi
boxers, sitting at the edge of his bed, looking at him with gleaming
eyes. Randolph didn't say a word. He just looked into Calvin's
eyes for what seemed an eternity, biting his lower lip with his pearly
white teeth. Calvin was entranced by Randolph's empathizing, yet
seductive stare. Calvin slowly turned over and laid his head back
on his pillow, never losing eye contact with Randolph. The gaze
was so intense that if he ever blinked, he didn't realize it. There
were no words, no sound, just silence and the communication of
eyes. Then, as if silently instructed, Calvin closed his eyes and sunk
further back into his pillow. He felt thick, soft lips brush his own
and a sensation like he had never felt coursed through his body. He
felt a wonderfully wet tongue emerge from the lips kissing his and
force an entrance into his mouth to begin a seductive dance with his
own tongue. Gradually Randolph withdrew his tongue and moved
his attention to Calvin's neck, licking from the start of his chest up
to his chin. Calvin's groans and tremors assured Randolph that
his actions were pleasing. As if he planned to taste every part of
Calvin's body, Randolph moved down and began first licking and
then nibbling at Calvin's erect protruding nipples. This was too
much for Calvin and his body began to shake almost uncontrollably
as hard breaths made their way out of him. Calvin was careful to
never open his eyes for fear this moment of unimagined pleasure
might end.

Everything came to a sudden stop as they both heard water
running in the single bathroom in the old house. Miss Letha
must be up getting ready to prepare breakfast. Randolph quietly
moved back over to the other bed, got under the covers and feigned
sleep.

Calvin lay absolutely still for a few minutes, his dick still as
hard as Chinese algebra and the crotch of his worn out briefs wet
with pre-cum. At this moment he hated Gran more than ever for

wonderful feeling he ever had. None of the
ida had shared, nor any of the sexual encounters
close to the ecstasy he felt this wonderful early fall

Chapter 6

Two months after their first visit to Woolfe as a couple, Esther asked Gran if it was o.k. to bring Randolph back home for Thanksgiving. Of course, Gran was delighted. She reveled in the fact that the ladies at Mt. Hope were still talking about how handsome and smart Randolph was. They had been floored when Gran interrupted church service on that Sunday when Randolph first made his appearance.

Gran stood up just as Sister Pope was finishing the announcements and said, "Brothers and sisters, I want you to meet my granddaughter's *friend* from school, Randolph. Randolph is just like a grandson to me now, and he's studying to be a *doctor*! Praise the Lord! When Esther brought this young man home this weekend to meet me, I knew that the Good Lord had helped me, an old lady, to raise these poor little fatherless children right so they could make good decisions." Gran shot a knowing eye at Esther as she said "good decisions."

The whole thing that Sunday had pissed Calvin off; but that was then. Now, Calvin was beside himself with excitement and anticipation. He did not know how to articulate even to himself what he felt, but he knew he had been counting the days until he saw Randolph again. He had convinced himself that nothing happened between them other than two guys "messing around" or experimenting, which was perfectly normal for young men who had established a friendship. He convinced himself that his excitement was for having a friend to talk to for a couple of days.

"Calvin, why don't you have a girlfriend?" Randolph asked.

They acted as though nothing had ever happened. However, Randolph and Calvin were off to bed much earlier than they normally would have been. Normally, on a Wednesday night before Thanksgiving, Calvin would have wanted to stay up until channel 3, the local television channel, had played the National Anthem and went to all static on the thirteen inch black and white TV. This night, Randolph said he was tired from the three hour drive and went into the boy's room as if he had grown up sleeping in that bunk bed. Calvin quickly followed awkwardly. Thank God Robert Jr. was stationed in Germany and of course would not be home for the holidays, imposing on Calvin's private time with Randolph in "their room".

Neither of them went to sleep but rather began the one-on-one conversation Calvin had been longing for all day.

"I don't know, I guess Gran is so hard on me that I figured she wouldn't let me spend any time with a girlfriend anyway," Calvin lied.

Actually he had no idea why the thought never crossed his mind. Even when he and Zelda were meeting and having sex, he never really felt that Zelda was his girlfriend. He knew he loved her, but she was not his "girlfriend".

"Man, you're a good looking cat. You ought to be able to get any girl at your school. Seems like you are wasting that playboy smile and jock body. What you doing to keep your body so toned anyway?"

"I do push ups every night and doing all this work around here keeps me in pretty good shape too. I hate that it's getting cold, I think wood chopping is in my very near future. My body is not all that though. You are the one who's in really good shape," Calvin replied.

"Man, I ran track all through high school and a little in college. That's how I got my first scholarship. My legs are big but I wish I had your upper body. Take your shirt off, let me see that chest."

On cue, Calvin flipped the white tee shirt over his head and onto the floor, leaving him exposed in only his boxer shorts that were really too small for him.

Randolph reached out and rubbed the backside of his hand across Calvin's tight, built chest as if it were nothing. At Randolph's touch, Calvin's dick immediately went hard. He wanted to try to conceal it but was afraid his efforts would only draw attention to it.

"Man, if I had your buff chest with these big legs, I would be ready! You gotta admit that these some fine legs, right?" Randolph questioned, half joking, half serious as he put his fine thigh across Calvin's lap.

Randolph repositioned his leg so that his calf lay directly on Calvin's hard dick. As Calvin tried hard to keep his dick from jumping against Randolph's leg, Randolph went on with the conversation as if nothing was wrong.

"Man, we need to go for a run together tomorrow. You think you can hang with me?" Randolph asked with a smirk.

"Man, I'll smoke you," Calvin retorted confident but playful.

"Oh see, you want to compete. I'm just trying to spend some Q' time with you bro," Randolph responded.

Becoming more serious Calvin asked, "So why do you want to spend quality time with me?"

"I've been thinking about you ever since we talked when I was here in September. I don't know, you kinda remind me of myself, Man. I think I understand you a lot better than anyone else and a lot more than you think." Randolph moved in a little closer as he spoke, allowing his leg to slowly glide across Calvin's still hard dick.

Then there was the stare; the erotic dance of the eyes that had kept Calvin awake for several nights after Randolph's last visit.

Calvin sat silent as Randolph simply looked into his eyes with the slightest suggestion of a smile on his face. And then it happened. Randolph, who had slid almost into Calvin's lap at this point, leaned in and gently kissed Calvin's thick pink lips with such sensuality that Calvin trembled on contact. These two together were as delicious as a chocolate and vanilla swirled ice cream cone.

Randolph moved his face down and took up where he left off when they were interrupted on that early morning in September. He began to first lightly lick around Calvin's nipples and then he moved in for the actual erect nipple itself, going from a gentle lick to all out biting. Calvin moaned in ecstasy, knowing he had to keep as quiet as possible, as not to wake Gran or Esther. Randolph moved his tall muscular body on top of Calvin's grinding his manhood against Calvin's as he resumed kissing him with deep deliberate tongue thrusts. Calvin thought he would explode feeling Randolph's body all over his; feet against feet, chest against chest, thighs against thighs, and most igniting of all, dick against dick. He knew this was a dangerous act and if anyone caught them, he had no idea what he would say or do; but he couldn't stop it. It felt too good, too right. Randolph moved his long arms down and pulled his own boxers off never allowing his lips to leave Calvin's. Then he licked his way down to Calvin's stomach and with the same stealth, removed Calvin's tight shorts while continuously licking and kissing him. Calvin was glad Randolph could accomplish this with such ease. He was afraid that if Randolph had paused for even a moment, he would have realized the danger of his actions and ended these acts of unprecedented pleasure.

"Damn!" Randolph exclaimed in a loud whisper when he took Calvin's shorts down and released his giant throbbing dick. He looked in wonder at its size for a moment and then without warning took all he could of it into his mouth. At that, Calvin actually grunted out loud. For a moment, both men lay perfectly still, listening to see if Calvin's noise had awakened anyone. Although Gran's little house was built during the years when homes were made solid and stable, the walls were still paper thin. Nothing stirred beyond the sounds of rustling fall leaves blowing in the night winds, squirrels dancing to the pleasure of being able to run free and undisturbed in the darkness, and whatever other small nocturnes ruled the woods in the night. They both eased with relief at the silence within the house and slowly, but surely, eased back into the rhythm they had begun.

Randolph continued to orally please Calvin until he could take it no longer and forcefully pulled Randolph's head up as a volcano of white lava violently erupted from him, barely missing Randolph's face. Calvin's whole body quivered in delight as he painstakingly gasped to regain his normal breathing. Randolph grabbed Calvin's tee shirt from the floor and handed it to him to clean himself as best he could, knowing there was no way he would be able to go to the bathroom and clean up at this time of night without everyone in the house waking to the sound of the running water.

As suddenly as it all had begun, it ended. Randolph simply climbed into the too small bunk bed and uttered not another sound. Calvin lay equally as silent to the observer, but inside his head there were sounds as loud as fire alarms going off. Although Calvin wiped himself dry to the touch, he could still feel the hot cum hitting his chest as it spit violently out of his own dick. The sour, salty smell of it invaded his nostrils. He was even afraid Gran would be able to smell it in her room a few yards away and inquire about the funny smell in the morning.

Chapter 7

Gran did not smell Calvin's cum, nor did anyone hear his grunts. The next morning, which was Thanksgiving morning, all was well... very well. Gran was moving about the warm kitchen like lightning, commanding Esther and Sarah as if the Queen were coming to dinner. By mid morning, the pungent odor of mustard greens and chitterlings, mixed with the sweet undercurrent of sweet potato pies and pound cakes had overtaken the entire house.

That autumn afternoon was perfect. A cool wind blew the dying leaves off the lazy trees making a giant color palate of the ground. Leaves all shades of orange, red, yellow, brown, and some still green were everywhere. Inside the small home, the scene was complimentary of the one outside. The smorgasbord of edible delights were comprised of the same color scheme as if planned... roasted hen and dressing, greens, green beans, field peas, corn, sweet potato and cherry pies, etc. Gran had Calvin and Randolph rearrange the plastic covered furniture in the living room to accommodate the old wooden square table from the kitchen. Gran had invited Mr. Broomfield whose wife had died, leaving him with five children ranging in ages from four to thirteen. The children would eat at the relocated table in the living room while the adults flanked the long table in the dining room.

The day was made even more wonderful for Calvin by his lingering afterglow from last night's dance with ecstasy and by his constant thoughts of Randolph. Every time his eyes met Randolph's, his heart beat a little faster. Every time he came within arm's reach of him, he actually felt a wave of heat climb his entire body. When they were moving the furniture, Calvin's dick went hard at the sight of Randolph's muscles flexing as he lifted.

Something within him told Calvin that his relationship with Randolph had somehow graduated. He was not sure into what, but whatever it was, it made him feel good. It had been a very long time since Calvin could remember being this happy. As a matter of fact, he could not remember a time in his life when he felt as genuinely happy as he did today. He could not rationalize why, but he felt that Randolph was now *his* Randolph. And though Esther brought him home, Randolph belonged to *him*. It reminded him of the time that Robert Jr. was given a puppy by a neighbor for helping him catch runaway cattle. The frightened puppy immediately took to Calvin and, though given to Robert Jr., it was understood that the puppy was Calvin's.

Dinner was fantastic. The long oak table had been draped with a dark fall patterned sheet. Each place at the table had been set with one of Gran's hand made laced dinner napkins and a setting of antique silverware. Dinner was served on China plates that had been given to Gran by her grandmother. Gran always assumed the china had been stolen from her great grandfather's former owner after he had been made a freed slave.

Around the table sat Mr. Broomfield, now widowed and elderly Reverend Mullin, Randolph, Esther, Sarah, Calvin, and Gran who had taken her throne at the head of the table. Calvin had subconsciously waited for Randolph and Esther to sit first so that he could be sure to sit next to Randolph.

Gran had other plans. "I want 'Randy' to come sit here by me." And with that order, Randolph took Esther's hand and they moved

27

so that he sat on the end next to Gran and Esther sat on the other side of him.

Calvin could not imagine why, but this slightly angered him. His annoyance at the fact that there was no seat by Randolph was compounded somehow by Gran's calling him "Randy." Where did she get off just making up a pet name for *his* pet? But refusing to have his wonderful day taken from him, he casually moved into the seat directly across from Randolph. The view was much better here anyway. So there, dilemma solved. What came next, he was not at all ready for.

After Reverend Mullin's ten-minute prayer thanking God for everything known to man, all that could be heard was the clanking of silver on china and the smacks of unsophisticated eaters. Every now and then Reverend Mullin would take a breath and utter, "Lord have mercy Ms. Letha! You put yo foot in this food!" With no consideration whatsoever for cholesterol, fat, sugar, or calories, everyone ate until there were only sighs of gluttonous misery.

As if startled into it, Randolph broke the silence in a voice uncharacteristically high pitched for him. "Excuse me! Can I get everyone's attention?"

After carefully looking to make sure everyone was listening, even the kids in the adjoining open living room, he continued.

"Esther and I have been going together for a few months now and in that time, I've come to know her wonderful family as my own. Gran has already adopted me as one of her grandchildren and Esther and I have decided to make it official. We're getting married!"

Gran jumped to her feet turning over the glass of sweet tea in front of her, praising God with every phrase of thanksgiving she could conjure up. "Glory Hallelujah! Thank you, Jesus! Lord, you done heard this old woman's prayers!"

Amidst all the hand shaking, back patting, and congratulatory hugs, Calvin sat stunned. His thoughts and emotions were in a whirlwind. The whole scene was surreal to him. Everything seemed to be in slow motion and all the sounds were loud, slurred, and very delayed. For the briefest of moments he thought he was losing his mind. He was first shocked, then hurt, then angry, very angry. And the worst part of all was that he didn't know why. He had no idea why it infuriated him more than he could stand to know that *his* Randolph had pledged his love to Esther. He could not fathom why he wanted to scream, turn the table over, and strangle someone to death. Most disturbing was the fact that it was Esther he wanted to strangle, not Randolph. His rational mind told him that he should be very happy for his sister. His remarkably mature understanding told him that this was a very good thing. But something inside of him would not let him celebrate this news. Something inside him told him this was a terrible thing and he began to feel the hurt.

Calvin watched the scene around him for what seemed to be hours, but actually was a couple of minutes, before he realized Gran was watching him. As he spread his lips into a smile to camouflage his feelings, he felt the sensation of his lower lip trembling as he moved it. Then, without warning, his eyes flooded right in front of Gran! Horrified, Calvin rose to rush from the room before anyone else noticed.

Gran grabbed his arm, "Calvin, it's o.k. boy. Sometimes when news is this good, it just makes you want to cry for joy. It don't make you no funny boy, it just mean you happy for your sister. When I think how good it's gonna feel telling all the ladies at the Women's Auxiliary meeting that I'm gonna have a doctor for my grandson, I just want to cry for joy too!"

Chapter 8

After the Thanksgiving announcement of Esther and Randolph's engagement, Calvin reverted to the same feelings of loneliness and abandonment he had been overcome with when Zelda left. On Thanksgiving night, Calvin retired to bed early and pretended to be asleep when Randolph came into the room. Even when Randolph sat on Calvin's bed and asked if he was alright, Calvin did not stir or open his eyes.

Shortly thereafter, Calvin got himself a job as a night cashier at Fill Up Market, the one gas station and convenience store that was open past ten o'clock in Woolfe. The store was the dingy little green hut with three gas pumps at the corner of 2nd and Main. It always carried the odor of old grease used to cook the ninety-nine cents chicken snack packs it was so popular for.

Fill Up's, as the locals knew it, was a franchised store owned by Bob Blackmon, a greasy haired, cantankerous, skinny white man in his early fifties with a cigarette perpetually hanging from the corner of his mouth. Although Mr. Blackmond was a pretty tall man, he walked and stood hunched over shorting himself by a foot. Bob Blackmon was trailer trash in a brick house. He and his wife, Effie, had poured the money they received from Effie's father's life insurance into buying into the southern convenience store chain.

For the first few weeks Calvin was there, Mr. Blackmon and fat Effie would drive slowly by the store several times to see if he was stealing or had friends hanging around the store keeping him from his work. Little did they know that Calvin had no friends. They paid Calvin minimum wage as a cashier, but gave him duties of a stock clerk, custodian, fried chicken cook, and store manager.

With his earnings from this miserable servitude, Calvin planned to buy himself a car for college. Gran, on the other hand, had other plans.

"You grown and working so you need to help out more around here. From now on, you need to pay for the groceries, lights, and gas bill," Gran demanded.

"But Gran, I only make enough to give Mr. Broomfield gas money for picking me up everyday after I put some money away for my car."

"*Yo car?* Boy, I'm talking bout paying these bills and you talking bout buying a car so you can run up and down the street and be a big shot?! You better get outta my kitchen with that mess."

Calvin had calculated that if he saved most of his check each week, he would have enough to buy a decent used car and some clothes for college by the end of the summer. Now, with Gran's mandate, he would only have enough for clothes and bus fare to Atlanta.

Calvin had been worried that he would not fit in on a college campus. He was also concerned about adjusting to living in a real city, and Atlanta in 1982 was becoming one of the larger cities in the South. Randolph had told Calvin that the sure way to fit in at College, especially a historically black college, would be to buy a car. Most students would not have cars because they were either too focused on their studies to have a job to afford one, or they were from big cities like New York or Chicago where people did not use cars much. Therefore, a student with a car would gain instant popularity and liking. Gran had effectively snatched yet another comfort from Calvin with her new policy.

Calvin could hardly contain his helpless fury knowing Gran had legally adopted him and his siblings and therefore collected State funded aid that more than covered his needs. He remembered how Gran threw a fit of anger when the government check had been reduced because Robert Jr. left home and joined the military. Moreover, Gran, as legal guardian and adoptive parent, was collecting the checks from their father's social security that came every month for Calvin and his two sisters who were still in college and eligible for disbursement. Yes, rearing the Sharpe children had become quite a lucrative racket for Gran. *And now she wanted more?*

Although he was no stranger to disappointment, this was one thing Calvin intended not to lose. Going to Atlanta in the fall without a car was not an option. He would make it happen, he just had to figure out a way to get the money without Gran knowing. Then he would wait until the last minute before he left to buy the car, or buy one in Atlanta. There had to be far more choices of used cars in Atlanta than the whole state of Mississippi combined. He decided that waiting only made sense.

As Calvin was finishing up his shift at Fill Up's a few nights later, his feet reminded him that he had been standing on a hard concrete floor constantly for over seven hours straight. Calvin began to feel a burning sensation in the balls of his feet as he walked. Although he usually only worked four or five hours, tonight he had been forced to come in earlier because Bob and Effie Blackmon were going out of town for the weekend and there was no one else they trusted in the store alone without them other than Calvin or Angie, and Angie was not willing to stay later than her usual shift. He was so anxious to get out of that store that he considered not even counting the drawers down and leaving it for Angie, the Blackmon's spoiled, lazy niece who officially held the title of manager; but his conscious weighed too great on him. So there he was, locked in the quiet store with all the outside lights off, sitting in the back office counting over a thousand dollars in mostly loose change and one dollar bills.

"Damnit! This is why I didn't want to count this drawer in the first place; I knew it would be short. I don't care how careful I am on my shift, that stupid Angie always leaves the drawer short from her shift," Calvin spoke aloud to himself.

Then the idea hit him like lightning. First as a "what if I dared" crazy thought. Then the idea took root and began to grow.

"What if I were very careful not to come up short on my shift and simply took five dollars from each shift? I could hide that money and Gran would never know." Calvin's face lit up as the plan developed in his mind. He stood over the bag of money representing the day's sales both frightened at the thought of actually taking money and excited at the idea of having the money he needed to buy his car.

Since the drawer was only nine dollars short, down from it's usual twenty to thirty dollars shortage, Calvin figured there was no time like the present to put his plan into motion. He looked around the dusty, dark back room space occupied mostly by eight tier racks of stocked merchandise. Calvin sat at the little scratched up desk and surveyed the musty room as if there was a possibility of someone magically appearing behind one of the racks of potato chip boxes. Calvin knew full well he had locked and bolted down both doors from the inside and there was no possibility of anyone getting in without breaking an alarmed window. Still his nerves were frazzled. Calvin took a crisp new twenty-dollar bill in his hand and stared at it for a few moments before folding it over and over until it was a small rectangle the size of a stick of gum. Calvin slowly moved the bill into the front pocket of his faded jeans. This single nervous action was the start of Calvin's hidden savings account.

Chapter 9

"I sure wish Robert Jr. was here to see you do your speech in front of all of Woolfe at the graduation Friday. Boy, I tell you I'm going to be so proud sitting up there in them bleachers when my grandson steps up to that pulpit as the salutatorian of the Class of 1982! A full year early 'cause he's so smart. I just can't wait to be sitting up there in my new red feathered hat to go with my red dress. I got red to match ya'll school colors." Gran was beside herself with anticipation as she shuffled around the kitchen fixing breakfast for her and Calvin.

"Gran, you don't have to match our school colors. Red is a little loud to be wearing I think. It's a podium, not a pulpit. And it's not that big of a deal for Junior to be coming home for. It's just a five minute speech," Calvin said nonchalantly sitting at the kitchen table, trying his best to not show his excitement and pride of his accomplishments.

"Well, it's a great big ole deal to me and all of this here Mt. Hope community. We ain't never had nobody to make no speeches at a white graduation before so yessir, this is a big ole deal to us. And yessir I will be sitting right down front wearing my red dress, red hat, and red shoes cause ain't nobody gonna miss seeing me tell everybody sitting round me that you is my grandson, the first colored boy to make one of these speeches at Woolfe High School."

Calvin shut his eyes and shook his head in dread of that moment. He was now afraid that Gran's actions and/or attire would completely throw his concentration and mess up his speech. He could see it now; Gran there, black as tar in all that bright red talking aloud while he was nervously trying to educate his classmates on the challenges of adulthood in the last couple of decades of the millennium.

As if she had forgotten to share some major information, Gran interrupted herself. "Oh! Sarah will be here Thursday, but Esther and Randolph won't get here until Friday evening, so they will just come straight to the graduation."

Calvin hadn't thought about Randolph for weeks, but now visions of their last encounter awakened in his memory. Calvin still was not sure how to explain what had happened between him and Randolph nor could he explain why he felt so betrayed at Randolph's proposal to Esther. All he knew was ever since that Thanksgiving Day announcement, his relationship with Randolph had not been the same. But Calvin was not about to let anything bother him right now. He was finally graduating, a year younger than the rest of his peers. Moreover, he had been named class salutatorian. Although his grade point average actually proved he should have been named valedictorian, there was no way the school officials at Woolfe High were going to let a black boy stand as the smartest student of the class. To top things off, Calvin had been able to stash away over five hundred dollars, the fruit of his frequent illegal withdrawals from the Fill Ups deposit bag. He kept this bundle of fives, tens and twenties in a manila envelope between his mattress and box spring. He counted the smelly crumpled bills almost daily but vowed not to spend one dollar of it until he went to Atlanta in August.

* * *

"Calvin, I know you graduate tomorrow and your mind is all over the place, but we need to talk about something serious."

As Mr. Blackmon spoke, Calvin's heart began to beat so loud and fast that he could actually hear it in his ears. For a moment, he could hear nothing but his heart beating. *Is this what 'surreal' means? When things start to kinda go in slow motion and even sounds are slurred like when you put your finger on a record to keep it from going the right speed.* Calvin was sure he would spend his biggest day, graduation day, in jail. *I knew taking that money was not a good idea and would catch up to me, but why now?*

"Calvin, Mrs. Blackmon has noticed that the sales and daily deposits have not matched for a while now, mainly on the days that you close after Angie."

"Oh Lord, is this really happening? Please Lord, don't let this be happening! Please let this be a really bad dream, a nightmare. Should I run? He could never catch me; and by the time the police get here, I'll be in the woods. But I don't have a car, they will surely catch me. And what about Gran? She'll kill me. What about graduation? Have I worked this hard just to not graduate? My whole future is ruined! Even when I get out of jail, maybe prison, I won't be able to get into any college with a criminal record."

"Calvin, are you paying me any attention Son? This is important. I love Angie, she's just like my own child, but I think she's taking unfair liberties with the cash around here. Mrs. Blackmon and I have talked to her about it and she denies it to the point of tears but I know better. I need you to start counting the drawer at the start of your shift to make sure it's right. Once it gets to the end of the night, it's too late for me to prove it's Angie. Hell, at that point, she could say you're taking the money. I think she got the message and will stop, but just in case, you count both register drawers and call me immediately if you're short. Can you do that for me?"

"What?" Calvin responded with a laugh of disbelief. "I mean, sure Mr. Blackmon."

"Also Calvin, I just wanted to say Mrs. Blackmon and I are real proud of you Son. I'm sure your people are real proud too. A lot of coloreds around here don't do well in the public school system but you make your people look real good."

Just as Calvin was feeling guilty for taking the money and allowing Angie's reputation to take the fall, Mr. Blackmon's backhanded, racist compliment snatched his confession from his lips.

"Thank you Mr. Blackmon for that encouragement. I can truly say that when you say things like that, I am inspired to be the most successful man I can be. You could never know how much I am really taking away from my experience working for you." Calvin smirked thinking of the stuffed envelope under his mattress.

Chapter 10

"Ladies and gentlemen, fellow graduates, faculty, and staff; today is a very proud day for me. I have overcome great obstacles while working through many disappointments, hurts, and lack of resources. Tonight is only the portal into our future as productive citizens and members of society. As we step through this portal, I am certain we will never be the same again. There is a great anticipation in the air that tomorrow's new day will bring things we have never seen nor imagined…"

On this beautiful May evening, there was a slight breeze blowing, carrying the scent of honeysuckles and freshly cut grass as Calvin stood proud and handsome in his red cap and gown, laden with gold honor student ropes, a state scholar's medal, and the medallion worn by the salutatorian. Never had he looked and felt so grown and proud of himself. The bleachers on the Jack Wallace Memorial Football Field at Woolfe High School were filled to overflowing with the proud faces of parents, family, and friends of tonight's graduates. Although he had the body of an adult at age 14, today at 16, graduating a year early, he was truly a man: an intelligent, confident, and beautiful man. However, Calvin could have never imagined how true the words of his speech were, for the events of tomorrow would indeed change his life forever.

Calvin woke late Saturday morning after being up past midnight with his sisters and Randolph. He lay in bed wondering if yesterday was all a dream. The excitement, the pats on the back, the tight proud hugs, the handshakes pressing folded tens, twenties, and even a one hundred dollar bill into his hand, the tears of joy and pride. This was all too good to be true.

"Calvin, if you don't get up and get this breakfast I made in *your* honor, I ain't never gonna cook nothing special for you no more." Gran's voice came booming through the door waking Calvin from his memories of last night.

Calvin jumped out of bed noticing that Randolph had already gotten up and made up the bunk bed. Calvin realized how exhausted he must have been since he didn't remember Randolph ever coming to bed at all. When he reached the kitchen, his face lit up with pleasure at the wonderful country breakfast spread Gran and his sisters had prepared. There were platters of scrambled eggs, bacon, ham, flapjacks piled high, homemade biscuits, homemade peach preserves, breakfast potatoes, a pitcher of orange juice, and the coffee pot on the stove. Calvin was especially impressed that there were no grits. He hated grits, and told Gran this, but she usually insisted on making them and complaining when he wouldn't eat any. Today, she made all his favorites, including coffee, which she never allowed him to drink before because, "coffee is for grown folks."

Although Calvin had slept until nine o'clock, everyone waited for him before they ate. Calvin finally felt loved, accepted, and that he was a part of a real family. This cloudy Saturday morning's breakfast was the best meal he ever had. The little house was once again filled with wonderful aroma, there were at least three conversations going on at once around the kitchen table, and although it looked like a rainstorm was coming, at the Sharpe family table the sun was shining brighter than ever before. Even Gran was in a good mood.

"Calvin, I hope you enjoy this meal. I know how you love a good breakfast and I wanted to fix you something special. Now, this is the second Saturday of the month so I'm taking the girls with me to the Daughter's of Zion meeting this evening." Sarah and Esther gave each other a look of sheer dread as Gran made this announcement that they obviously knew nothing about.

"That means you and Randolph gonna have to have dinner alone today. I'll leave you something to eat but don't mess with them cakes on that counter, they're for the meeting. Them ladies just love Miss Letha's cakes," Gran said with a grin of utter pride before quickly refocusing her attention.

"So do we have a wedding date yet?" Gran directed her question to Esther and Randolph.

"Miss Letha..." Randolph began.

"*Gran...*" Gran corrected him.

He began again, "Gran, Esther and I have decided to wait a little while. We both will be graduating in the fall and we just want to get started working and save a little money first."

Gran's disapproval was obvious. She wanted this marriage and she wanted it right away.

"Sounds like backing out talk to me. You not trying to back out on us are you, Son?" Gran quizzed with obviously fake cordialness.

"Of course not. Gran you know I love this family and I love Esther. I promise you we will get married. We just want to make sure the time is right." Randolph's voice shook as if he had been threatened.

Calvin ate his food in silence as if his mind was a million miles away.

The rain continued all day and there was a coolness reminiscent of March or April, not at all the usual late spring-early summer heat of May. The smell of the rain was fragrant, carrying the mixed scent of wildflowers and muddy clay dirt. Calvin usually hated days like this. Usually, the rain would bring a heavy drowsiness upon him and he hated dragging around too sleepy to read or do anything productive. But today, today was different. The rain was not depressing or sedating, today it was beautiful. The rain reminded Calvin of the time God caused the rain to wash away all the sin and filth of the earth so that Noah and his family could create a new beginning. In his mind, this was Calvin's new beginning.

"Come on girls, we're gonna be late!" Gran stood by the door in a powder blue dress with tiny pink roses scattered here and there, her Sunday black purse, and black block heeled shoes. It was obvious by her impatient tone that Gran was not playing with Sarah and Esther. She was beside herself this weekend. First Calvin making a speech before what seemed to be the whole County, and now she would take her two college student granddaughters to show off to the ladies of Mt. Hope. Life didn't come much better than this to Gran.

As the entire house was left with only testosterone, Calvin and Randolph were alone for the first time since Randolph's proposal to Esther. Calvin immediately began to feel the awkwardness of the situation as they sat on opposite sides of the round table.

"This is my first chance to talk to you Cal. You excited about going to college in a few months?" Randolph asked, trying to break the ice.

"Of course man, I can't wait." Calvin gave a quick answer with no emotion in his tone.

"Cool. So Esther says you are going to do the Pre-Med track. Do you plan to specialize when you finish and go to medical school, or just do the General Practice thing?" Randolph was determined to make a conversation.

"Not sure yet," Calvin said, never lifting his eyes from his plate.

Randolph stared at Calvin solemnly for about a minute and out of nowhere hardened his voice to a low, deliberate tone. "What the hell is wrong with you?"

Startled, Calvin finally made eye contact with Randolph. "What? What are you talking about?"

"You know what I'm talking about. You have been treating me like I stole from you or something for a few months now. What's wrong with you? What did I do to you?" Randolph questioned with more sincerity than Calvin was used to.

"Nothing," still short answers from Calvin.

"Calvin, I am not crazy. You talk around me to other people, but you haven't spoken one word directly *to* me since Christmas; maybe even since Thanksgiving."

At that, Calvin abruptly rose and began to walk away. "Just put the dishes in the sink, I'll wash them before Gran gets home later." Calvin left the room as if this conversation had never happened.

Randolph followed Calvin to his bedroom where he found him laying face down on his bed, face stuffed in his pillow.

"You know what, Calvin? You're not gonna just dismiss me like that."

Calvin could tell Randolph was serious but he didn't care. He was not about to open up to him again to be betrayed again.

"Randolph, I don't have a problem with you man. Everything is *fine*." Calvin tried to sound casual talking muffled through his pillow.

"Wait a minute. You got upset when I said you hadn't talked to me since Thanksgiving. That's when me and Esther got engaged. Calvin do you *not* want me to marry your sister? Man, don't play that 'protective brother' role with me. You know I wouldn't do anything to hurt your sister. I…"

"Shut up! Shut up! Shut up!" Calvin fired the words in rapid succession as he sprung his head up staring at the wood paneled wall.

He continued, not even noticing the flood of tears that seemed to instantly emerge from his eyes. "I don't give a damn about protecting Esther from you. *I* need you, not Esther. Esther has her friends and Sarah. Gran loves Esther. Who do *I* have? What am I supposed to do now? You came here, making me feel like I finally had somebody for me; somebody to listen to me; somebody to care about me; somebody to make me feel special. Then after you touch me that way, you say that? *'Me and Esther are getting married,'* what kind of shit is that?"

Calvin's entire face was now wet with tears and mucous. His words trailed into a childlike hiccupping cry.

Randolph, now silently crying too, hesitated a moment then slowly sat on the side of Calvin's bed. He cupped one of his long hands on Calvin's shoulder and carefully but forcefully pulled him out of his pillow and turned him over onto his back. Randolph looked into Calvin's wet eyes for a few moments then lowered his face to Calvin's and kissed him. At first he kissed him gently on his thick pink lips, tasting the salt of his tears. Then he opened his mouth and parted those full lips with his tongue, snaking it artistically into Calvin and allowing the full length of it to fill Calvin's mouth.

Calvin closed his eyes in pleasure as he drifted from earth to the world he had visited a couple times before; trips he took with Randolph as his tour guide. Calvin had subconsciously longed for this pleasure since Thanksgiving. He did not understand that his anger, sadness, and confusion were indeed longing, longing for Randolph's touch. Although he had vowed to never allow Randolph to touch him again, he wanted it too bad and did not have the strength to fight it.

Randolph pulled away and slowly began to first undress Calvin and then himself. Calvin cooperated by going limp and allowing Randolph to pull his Honor Club tee over his head and slightly lifted his lower body as Randolph pulled off his worn jeans and white cotton boxers. Calvin's huge dick was hard and bobbing up and down in horny spasms. Randolph hungrily took all he could of it into his mouth, vigorously pumping his lips up and down on it loving the bittersweet taste of the pre-cum on his tongue. Calvin twisted and moaned in utter ecstasy trying his best to hold back his climax. Randolph, knowing Calvin could take no more, relaxed his oral grip and moved on to explore other areas. Randolph snuggled his head between Calvin's legs and licked his inner thighs, which caused him to jump at the surprising pleasure. Calvin had no idea that the sensations he was experiencing existed. Never in a million years would he even imagine that the simple act of placing a wet warm tongue on the spot between his testicles and his butt would feel so good. But Randolph seemed to instinctively find unexplored areas on Calvin with each passing minute.

After Randolph had buried his head as far as he could between Calvin's legs, he took Calvin's left leg in his strong hand and lifted it up and over, causing Calvin to twist at the waist, and flip over onto his stomach. Randolph, without thought or hesitation, pushed his face into Calvin's butt parting his cheeks with his tongue. At this, Calvin groaned out loud in obvious pleasure he had never expressed. Randolph took the cue and set up camp, licking and probing his tongue as far as he could get it into Calvin's pulsating hole. He could smell the cheap soap Calvin had bathed with just before dinner and could taste its bitterness at first, but he didn't care. Calvin spread his legs as far apart as he could, inviting Randolph to dig and find treasure.

Calvin's whole body seemed to be stimulated by the pleasures of one spot. He wanted this to last forever, but it didn't. After a few minutes, Randolph stopped. Calvin lay on his stomach wondering if Randolph had climaxed and was done, or if he wasn't enjoying it as much as he himself was and had just stopped. He could feel Randolph get up and walk over to the dresser. Calvin dared not speak or even lift his head to look at Randolph; he would not know what to say. Surprisingly, he walked back over to the bed and Calvin could feel him kneeling behind him. Calvin could hear a cap open, something squirting, and Randolph apparently rubbing something on himself.

Calvin was a little confused, but then remembered that one day he heard some of the guys at school saying that if you use lotion when you masturbate, it makes it easier and more intense. He just hoped that Randolph would pick up where he left off with his tongue. He did. This time Calvin did not flinch as Randolph's now familiar tongue entered his hole. It was warm and very very welcomed as Calvin's rim expanded and contracted around Randolph's tongue. After a few thrusts, Randolph lifted his head and seconds later Calvin felt very warm slippery flesh first massaging the area around his hole. Then there was pressure and he could feel Randolph on top of him kissing his shoulders and neck. Slowly Randolph's dick entered him, taking his breath away.

Calvin could keep silent no longer, "Shit!" he cried out in both pain and pleasure.

Randolph just began to move his dick in and out of Calvin like a water pump. At each entrance and exit, Calvin felt less pain and more pleasure. He knew he could not take this much longer, but loved knowing that Randolph was inside him. Randolph began to move faster and faster, the hard sniffs and breaths from his nostrils hitting Calvin's wet neck. All of a sudden, Randolph snatched his dick out of him. Calvin could feel burning spots of wetness squirting on his back as Randolph gripped one of Calvin's muscular butt cheeks tight in his hand grunting like he was trying to loosen a tight lid on a jar.

"What the *hell* is going on in here!"

Calvin's heart stopped as Randolph tumbled onto the floor scrambling for his clothes. It was Gran! This had to be a nightmare Calvin thought. He slowly turned over and there she was, hands on her wide hips with a look of murder in her eyes. Calvin disregarded Randolph's liquid running down his back as he sat up and pulled his knees to his chest in a poor effort to hide his nakedness.

"I don't even want to know what you two were just doing. In all my years I have never seen anything like this. Thank the good Lord I had Sister Pope bring me back, instead of Esther, to get the cake I forgot. This would break poor Esther's heart." Gran's voice trailed off into tears. She sighed a heavy breath and steadied herself against the doorframe biting her balled fist.

Gran looked at a blank spot on the floor for a silent eternity. Then, without looking up, she finally spoke in a mechanical, emotionless voice.

"Randy, get yourself cleaned up and put your clothes on. You should have never let this *thing* trick you, but the devil is cunning so I don't blame you for being weak. Now we just need to make sure Esther doesn't find out about this terrible mistake."

At this, Calvin came to life. "*Thing?* Did you call me a *thing?*"

"Shut your mouth in my house! You are an abomination before God and no kin to me." Gran's tone was low as she spoke each word with deliberate emphasis.

She continued, "Pack all the clothes you can take tonight and get the hell out of my house and out of Woolfe. I don't ever want to see you around here again. I'm gonna take this damn cake back to the church and when I get home, I'm gonna find out that you ran away all of a sudden. Do you understand me?"

When Gran's eyes finally met Calvin's, there was a look of utter disgust and hate in them. Calvin felt a chill all over his still naked body.

As she turned to walk away, back still turned, she calmed her voice to a cool, almost cordial tone, "Randy, when we get back I think we should sit down and plan out the wedding. If we have it in August, that gives us three whole months to get everything ready. I think that's all the time we'll need."

"Yes Ma'am," Randolph's childishly frightened reply.

Chapter 11

The huge bus reeked of a mixed odor of musty feet, cigarettes, wet dogs, and cherry flavored air freshener. As Calvin pressed his body as close to the window side of the bus as he could, he stared out the window, watching blurs of the Mississippi pines barely visible through the downpour of rain. The bus stopped in every little town from Woolfe to Jackson. Once he changed buses in Jackson and boarded the express, the only stops would be in Meridian, Birmingham and finally Atlanta. Before they reached Jackson, Calvin prayed every time the bus pulled off the highway that this would be the final destination of the fat white lady in the seat next to him so he could unplaster himself from the window.

Calvin knew he was in for a rough ride when he boarded the bus outside the Dixie Snack Shop and saw that the only seat in the non-smoking section of the bus was with this large pink blob of a woman in a flowered polyester dress. Her eyes were closed and a small gap evoked a slight whistle as she inhaled and exhaled through her nap. Calvin cleared his throat loudly to get her attention to no avail and finally had to tap her on the shoulder to wake her. The only good thing was the fact that throughout the entire hour and a half ride to Jackson, not one word passed between Calvin and the lady. The thudding beads of the rain and the rough engine of the bus were the only sounds Calvin heard the whole way.

Calvin attempted to sleep away his pain but the vibration of the window, coupled with the overwhelming smell of smoke, kept him awake. Calvin had always hated the smell of cigarette smoke and now wondered what was the point of smoking and non-smoking sections on a bus. There were no real partitions so the smoke would gather at the back of the bus for a few moments but simply make it's way throughout the whole bus as the blasting air conditioning fanned it around. The smoker might as well be sitting in the seat next to him.

The bus reached Jackson shortly after midnight on that rainy Saturday night. Calvin entered the big bus station in amazement. He had only been to Jackson a couple of times on trips with the Honor Club, but had never actually experienced the excitement of the city. Calvin was surprised to see a building so large dedicated solely to catching and getting off buses. There were video games, a diner, and chairs with TV's attached right to them. The layover would be two hours, so Calvin took a seat at one of the TV chairs and dug in his pocket for the twenty-five cents it required.

As the black and white rerun of *The Three Stooges* played before him, his mind began to think back on the events of the day. It seemed impossible that less than twelve hours ago, he had been at the highest point of his life and now he was at his lowest. The tears he had been fighting and holding all evening now began to trickle down his face. Calvin could see the scene of himself silently throwing as many clothes as he could carry in the ragged bright orange vinyl suitcase he took from beneath Gran's bed. He could see Randolph just sitting on the other bed watching in silence as he lifted his mattress and retrieved the manila envelope filled with five, ten, and twenty dollar bills, totaling over five hundred dollars he had taken from the convenience store. Even now, Calvin could feel the budge of bills he had removed from the envelope, rolled tight, and stuffed in his front pocket.

All that Calvin could think to do was head for Atlanta. He had no idea what he would do when he got there, or where he would stay. In August, he would be able to move into a dorm room at Morehouse, but it was only May. What would he do until then?

"You o.k. Sweetie?" Calvin was jolted back to the present by the unusually low toned voice of a lady who he had not noticed in the TV chair next to him. She was a very tall, thin, black lady who wore way too much make up, but was dressed flawlessly in a red dress, red high heels, red sequined purse, and red fingernails to match. The dress was gathered in the middle by an obviously fake and over-the-top jeweled broach. Her eyelashes were an inch long, jet black, and fluttered just a little too much. The woman made Calvin nervous. He wondered if he was experiencing his first conversation with a prostitute. Calvin simply nodded his head in answer to the lady's question.

"You look about as comfortable as a turkey at Thanksgiving. This your first time traveling alone, Baby?"

"Yes Ma'am," Calvin replied.

Laughing, the lady responded, "You don't have to call me Ma'am. I ain't that damn old. You cute as hell, Sweetie. Where you headed and why you sitting here crying?"

"I'm going to Atlanta and I've just had a pretty bad day. I'll be o.k." Calvin felt himself getting more comfortable with this lady. She was pretty funny.

"Well I'm Lavender, Lavender Chiffon. I'm going to Atlanta too. I live there."

"Calvin Sharpe. Pleased to meet you, Miss Chiffon. That's a really *unique* name." Calvin gave the lady a firm handshake.

"Whoa Sweetie! Don't break Miss Lavender's wrist. Darling, you don't have to prove you a man to me like that. I have other ways you can show me if you want though," Lavender suggested with a wink and exaggerated laugh. Calvin was amused at how she referred to herself in the third person.

At that point the overhead speakers came to life producing a mechanical female voice that was barely understandable. Calvin and Lavender turned their heads as if they would be able to make out the announcement better if their ears were tilted at an angle.

When Lavender made out the words *"Meridian"*, *"Birmingham"*, and *"final destination Atlanta"*, she stood and began walking away with purpose. Almost as an afterthought, she turned back to Calvin and said, "Come on, this is us, Sexy."

Calvin grabbed his orange suitcase he had carried on the bus with him rather than checking it underneath, and hurried behind Lavender as she click-clacked her high heals across the filthy tile floor, long silky black hair bouncing as her hips swayed seductively.

As the bus pulled out of the Birmingham terminal after an unreasonably long layover and bus delay, Calvin finally began to feel the excited anticipation of actually going to a big city for the first time in his life. The wait in Birmingham would have been unbearable had Lavender not been there. For the whole four hours they waited, Lavender picked out one person after another in the bus terminal to make jokes about... *"Baby, what bird nested in that wig?" "Now there's a man with a huge dick!" "It's amazing how they got that monkey to walk and talk like that."* Calvin couldn't remember laughing so hard in his whole life. He instantly liked Lavender although there was definitely something a little different about her. Her wit and overbearing personality totally took his mind off Woolfe, Gran, and Randolph.

"So Sexy, what you going to do in Atlanta when you get there?" Lavender asked.

"I'm not really sure. School starts in the fall but I guess I hadn't thought about what I'm going to do until then." A panic began to grip Calvin's chest as he uttered the words. Where would he stay? He had his money still waded in his pocket but how long would it last? How much would a hotel room cost in big city like Atlanta? What kind of job could he get being a county boy with no real skills other than running a country store?

"Well baby, you better start thinking about it, because I've seen Atlanta swallow up cuties like you. With your looks, you could definitely make some money but I don't want you to get involved with that stuff. You're a good kid and there is more out there than you've ever imagined in your wildest, horniest thoughts. Don't go looking to find out how much you can do without doing too much. I'm telling you from experience, you never know you've gone too far until you look around and can't find your way back."

"I don't think that will happen to me, Lavender. I have a plan and I'm focused." Calvin threw his response back as he looked out the window at a changing new South passing outside.

Two hours and twenty minutes later, as the big blue and white bus with the running dog on it entered Atlanta on I-20, Calvin's heart began to race. Exit signs with street names were a delicacy to him. Back in Woolfe, there had only been a few streets with names in the entire town. All the other roads were dirt or rock and were just known by location, "*...go to the third road past the big pecan tree,*" "*the curvy road where there's a brown house on the right,*" "*turn at the 'Buy Peaches Here' sign.*" But not here. Calvin saw Thornton Road and Fulton Industrial Blvd., and as they got closer into the city he thought he would jump up out of his seat. There it was, the Atlanta skyline. It was the most wonderful thing he had ever seen. Tall buildings lit up the night sky like Christmas. He imagined the thousands, tens of thousands, and even hundreds of thousands of people working in offices, eating in restaurants, riding elevators, riding in taxis, having coffee in coffee shops, and just generally being city folk. This is what he wanted; he wanted to be city folk. He wanted to walk on sidewalks and see people he did not know and have no obligation to smile and speak if he did not want to. He wanted to go to church if he felt like it, but if he didn't, just go and have Sunday breakfast in a quaint little restaurant. He wanted to have friends who would throw parties where everyone would sit around eating delicate little dishes and drinking out of fancy stemmed glasses discussing good books and current events. Even at his very young age, Calvin longed to be metropolitan.

"Wow," Calvin could not help but whisper.

"There she is, Miss Atlanta, Honey," Lavender replied as she woke from a quiet nap.

She continued to speak as she folded her thin brown blanket and tucked it through her purse straps, "She's the new Queen of the South. This city has grown like wildfire over the past few years. It's because of Maynard Jackson. That man is what you call a visionary. I just hope these fools have enough sense to put Andy Young in office this fall to finish some of the good things Mayor Jackson has started. You make sure you get signed up to vote for him. I got friends in important places and they think that if we keep growing like this, we can be like New York or Chicago in the next ten or twenty years. We already have about two million people in all the metro. Who knows, we may have five million one day! I know, I'm dreaming but I love me some Atlanta baby. Don't get me started."

Lavender seemed to come alive talking about Atlanta and it's promising future. This talk made Calvin even more exited. He could only imagine living in a city with Black mayors and millions of people.

"Lavender, what were you doing in Jackson? What could ever make you leave this city?"

"Oh baby, I was doing a show. I travel all over the place working, but my home is Atlanta. I'll die here."

"A show? You're a singer or something?" Calvin asked innocently.

"Oh Doll, you are so sweet; so sweet and so dumb. I'm an entertainer. That's all you need to know now. One day you'll get it, one day real soon walking around with that body in Atlanta."

Calvin just continued looking out the window bewildered by Lavender's comments.

As the bus abandoned the highway and snaked it's way through the city, Calvin tried to read every sign they passed. Jewelry stores, pawnshops, barbershops, shoe stores, delicatessens, and cafés all passed by.

"Do you know where you're staying yet?" Lavender asked.

"I saw a hotel just down that street. I'll go there tonight and then go over to the campus tomorrow to see if I can start school this summer and move into the dormitory," Calvin replied.

"Boy, you can't afford that hotel. You gonna have to go to a *motel*, with a '*m*'. Try that Budget Motel down off Spring. You can probably stay there pretty cheap until you get it figured out." Lavender advised.

As Calvin and Lavender parted ways at the bus station, Lavender gave Calvin a tight hug and pressed a note in his hand with her telephone number on it.

"Baby, this a big city full of vultures and you're a sweet beautiful boy. You be careful and call Miss Lavender if you need anything."

With that, she strolled down Forsythe Street with urgent purpose as if she were queen of the city.

Chapter 12

The Budget Motel was an old yellow five story building in downtown Atlanta. The flashing sign above the building had lights out and therefore gleamed "Bu get otel" in bright red neon. Calvin stepped out of the pre-summer night and approached the black laminate front desk of the hotel.

"Can I help you?" The middle aged, plump black lady behind the counter asked.

"I need a room for tonight... and maybe a few nights more. But I'll know that after I go to the school tomorrow and see if they'll let me move into the dormitory early," Calvin replied nervously.

"Son, I don't really need to know your life story. I just need thirty dollars a night and a copy of your driver's license or a credit card. Now do you want smoking or non smoking?"

"I want non smoking please, but I don't have a drivers license yet." Calvin began to worry that this wouldn't go as smoothly as he had hoped.

"Baby, how old are you? You got to be eighteen and have some sort of picture ID to stay here."

As the plump lady whose nametag read, "Verlina" empathetically explained this fact to Calvin, a young thin black man walked out from a hidden door to the desk with a hand full of papers. He hesitated for a minute, looked at Calvin, and then without a word returned to the hidden world behind the front desk wall.

"Ma'am, I don't have any ID and I'm sixteen, but I've graduated from high school. I am going to college here soon and just need somewhere to stay until I get my housing straightened out with the school. I don't have anywhere to go." Calvin's voice began to tremble as he pleaded.

"Son, I'm sorry, but I'm not going to get in trouble with my job. I don't really know what to tell you. Maybe you should go back home until you have somewhere at school to stay."

"I don't have a home," Calvin said as he snatched his orange suitcase up and walked out the door.

As Calvin reached the corner, not knowing what to do or where to go, he heard a male voice calling out.

"Hey man!" It was the man with the papers from behind the wall.

He continued when he knew he had Calvin's attention, "Verlina is from the old school and kind of set on policies and stuff. Her shift ends in ten minutes and then I'm here alone. Hang out here for about fifteen minutes then come in and we'll get you a room. I'm not about to let you be out here on these streets by yourself all night."

Calvin couldn't have been more excited if he were invited by the Queen to spend the night in Buckingham Palace. The fifteen minutes seemed to take hours to pass. In the absence of the old Timex watch he had accidentally left on the dresser at Gran's as he rushed out, he measured time by the digital clock on the bank building down the street.

Calvin gave it five extra minutes to be sure Verlina was gone and entered the hotel cautiously. He did not want the plump lady to become aggravated and call the police on him for not leaving. His heart lifted when he saw the nice young man at the counter alone beckoning him in.

"Come on in, Man. It's o.k. It's pretty much just you and me in this lobby alone," the man said with a smile.

"Now, we gonna get you a room, but you got to tell me what you doing down here by yourself at this time of night. It's obvious that you didn't really plan this trip. So did you run away or get kicked out?" The young man said still smiling warmly. He seemed to come alive once Verlina left.

"I had to leave home all of a sudden. My grandmother and I had a disagreement," Calvin said. He wanted to tell the whole story. He desperately needed to talk to someone about Gran and Randolph. He wanted to ask someone to explain what happened between him and Randolph, but he knew whatever happened, it was not something that you tell others. It was so terrible that it made Gran put him out so he didn't dare tell anyone else.

"It's o.k. man, and it's going to stay o.k. I heard you tell Verlina that you were gonna try to move on campus tomorrow. I got to tell you man, I don't think it's that simple but you can try. I'm working tomorrow night at the same time if you need to come back. I'm going to give you a discount so the room is only twenty dollars. By the way, I'm Darnell."

"Thanks so much Darnell. I definitely won't forget how you helped me." Calvin couldn't stop smiling, exposing the pearly white teeth behind his thick pink lips.

The next day Calvin, with step by step written instructions in his hand, boarded his first MARTA (Metropolitan Atlanta Rapid Transportation Authority) train and found his way to the Morehouse College campus. It was everything he imagined it would be. The quest for knowledge seemed to be in the air all around him. He felt his intelligence increase just being on the campus. He wandered the grounds for over an hour before finding the Housing Office. Once he found the right desk and waited half an hour to see someone and present his request, his fears were confirmed.

"I'm sorry, Mr. Sharpe. We just don't have any work study jobs available and it is too late to register for summer classes. I'm afraid

you're going to have to wait until August and come see us again."
The skinny lady with horn rimmed glasses smiled motherly as she
broke the bad news.

Calvin could not remember ever being called "Mr. Sharpe"
before. He was somewhat stunned at the sound of it. The rest of
the lady's speech faded into the background after the words, "Mr.
Sharpe". At those words, it became real to Calvin that he now,
at sixteen years of age, had to be a man; a real man totally and
singularly responsible for himself. It was up to him and him alone
to figure out how he would survive until August. Even with the
discount Darnell could give him, he would not be able to stay at the
hotel more than a week or two before running out of money.

Chapter 13

"Baby, I told you to call me if you needed me and damn if you didn't take me up on it!" Lavender exclaimed with laughter when she heard Calvin's story. Lavender had a way of making light of heavy problems that could only come from someone who has been forced to carry a lot of heavy weights in her lifetime. Calvin had been in Atlanta for over a week and his money was almost gone. He had nowhere else to turn.

"Well, I guess Ms. Lavender is gonna have to find another male child in the Promised Land somewhere to lay his pretty head. Lucky for you that a few people owe me favors. We just need to find one with an extra room until August." Then after a quiet hesitation, "Oh I know! I'll send you over to stay with Paul, but you got to promise me you won't let him talk you into doing nothing crazy. He has always been nice around me, but I hear he's showin' out a little these days." Lavender's voice took on a warning tone.

"Showing out like what? And how do you know he will let me stay?" Calvin asked skeptically.

"Don't worry about that, Sweety. If I want you to stay, you can stay. Do you know who I am?" Again there was Lavender's now familiar throaty giggle.

The next day, Calvin got the call in his hotel room from a low talking man named Paul. It was past midnight and Calvin was fast

58

asleep and startled by the phone. The man did not have a southern accent at all. His voice reminded Calvin of the men he had seen on the TV shows in the hotel room. He occasionally ran across a few guys in Atlanta who spoke like this. Darnell explained that these were guys who had moved from the "East Coast" to Atlanta in hopes of a slower, better life.

Paul told Calvin he would pick him and his orange suitcase up on Friday and they would work out the financial arrangements later. Calvin was embarrassed that Lavender had apparently made fun of his suitcase when talking to Paul. Calvin offered to give him the little money he had on Friday, but Paul told him to keep it until they discussed rent. Calvin was relieved, knowing that by Friday, he would have little or no money left anyway.

Darnell had been feeding Calvin daily with food he could get for free from the café adjacent to the hotel. He had proven to be a good friend to Calvin, but even with all his help, Calvin was still sinking fast. His search for a job had been fruitless. Without a driver's license, birth certificate, or parental consent, no employer took his application seriously.

Calvin stood nervously on the sidewalk outside the Budget Motel with his orange suitcase sitting between his knees. Calvin had heard the stories of theft in big cities and wanted to be able to feel the suitcase touching him at all times for fear someone would come by and swoop it up unbeknownst to him. Calvin laughed to himself at the thought that in all his life, he had never heard of anyone in or around Woolfe ever being robbed.

Paul had called Calvin the previous night and told him he would pick him up outside the hotel at five thirty. When Calvin asked Paul how he would recognize him, he said, "Don't worry man, I'll know you when I see you."

Sure enough, at five forty five, a shinny new silver Mercedes-Benz slowed to a smooth stop in front of Calvin. He would have never imagined that this beautiful luxury car could belong to the man coming for him. Calvin had only seen cars like this on TV or passing quickly on the streets of Atlanta, and never in Woolfe.

"Calvin?" The peanut butter brown man said. White teeth gleaming as he spoke.

"Yes sir," Calvin responded nervously.

"Oh Man. Please don't call me Sir. I'm Paul and I guess I'm gonna be your landlord for a minute. Get in, let's go."

The trunk popped by itself which startled Calvin and he placed his suitcase in it. Then he came to the front passenger door and carefully opened it, trying not to get his fingerprints on the handle. He sat upright as if he was too dirty to touch the seat.

Paul was a little shorter than six feet tall and small framed although one could tell he worked out with weights from time to time. He was very well groomed with a neatly trimmed mustache and goatee, and low haircut. Paul wore a brown polo shirt a few shades darker than his own skin neatly tucked into khaki trousers. He was obviously in his late twenties or early thirties.

"Man, get comfortable. Sit back. Don't be nervous, I won't hurt you." Paul flashed a million dollar smile that set Calvin at ease and he leaned back as they took 20 East out of the city to the new developing area of Stone Mountain. In one of their late night conversations after all the other hotel employees went home, Darnell had mentioned that Stone Mountain was quickly becoming an area where affluent black people were beginning to build nice homes.

Paul seemed a lot friendlier in person than on the phone. He pretty much stated the facts on the phone, but now was cordial and helped Calvin get over the feeling of being a burden or charity case.

Paul's house was a nice ranch style three-bedroom home on a quiet tree-lined street in Stone Mountain. As they pulled into the drive, Paul hit a wide button on a box attached to his sun visor and the garage door begin to roll back. As the garage door rose, so did Calvin's excitement which was made apparent by his widening eyes.

No one in Woolfe had a garage, no one. A few had "car ports" or sheds where they housed their cars, but no electronic doors attached right onto the house.

Wide-eyed and mouth open, Calvin walked into the house as if into an absolute mansion. Paul had decorated the whole house with leather; white leather furniture, leather masks and wall art; and a white leather bar filled one corner of the living room. A stone-faced fireplace completely covered the far wall of the split-level living room. Calvin was in utter amazement.

"Let me show you your room," Paul said with great pride. He could read Calvin's expression like a second grade textbook.

The room where Calvin would sleep was a fully furnished bedroom. Everything in the room was red and black down to the black lacquer dresser and night stands.

"This is your home kid. Make yourself comfortable," Paul said with an air of sincerity.

After taking everything out of his suitcase for the first time since he left Woolfe, Calvin sat on the soft bed and finally breathed a sigh of relief. He had been to hell and back and it felt good to have somewhere safe, comfortable, and even luxurious to call home. Although the traffic was the worst Calvin had ever seen and it seemed to take hours to get home, it was still relatively early. So Calvin went back into the living room where Paul was watching the news on TV. Calvin noticed, as he entered the room, the sweet scent of vanilla throughout the house. He assumed the smell was coming from the many candles that had been lit in and around the fireplace.

"Hey Calvin. You getting acclimated to your new home?" Paul asked.

"Yes, thank you. You have a very nice home." Calvin was still not quite comfortable in casual conversation with Paul.

"Calvin, don't be so formal with me man. And at least for a little while, you can say *we* have a nice home."

In response to that warm reply from Paul, Calvin flashed his sunshine-on-a-rainy-day smile and joined Paul on the white sofa.

"You want a cocktail?" Paul asked. Calvin noticed that Paul held a small glass half filled with an orange colored liquid.

"Oh, no thanks." He was too embarrassed to say that he didn't really know what a "cocktail" was.

"Are you even old enough to drink legally? How old are you?" Paul asked.

"Sixteen. I'll be seventeen in a couple of months." Calvin responded as if ashamed of his youth.

"Sixteen! Are you kidding? You just a kid, but you look like a grown man. How the hell are you supposed to be going to college this fall?" Paul was incredulous.

"I skipped a year in school because of my grades. I developed early mentally and physically. My grandmother told me that my father grew up really fast too. I guess it's hereditary. Hopefully I won't follow too closely in his footsteps and die early too." Calvin tried to pass the comment off lightly.

Calvin began to loosen up and found himself talking more and more and genuinely enjoying the conversation with Paul. He learned that Paul was thirty-two, had moved to Atlanta from New York in the seventy's fresh out of college. He was a sales executive with a large paper company now and seemed to be living out his dream. Calvin also learned that Paul loved his "cocktails"; during the course of the conversation, he had emptied six glasses.

"How do you know Lavender?" Calvin asked.

"She spotted me out at a show and actually came up to me and sat on my lap and did part of her act with the spotlight on us. I was so embarrassed and pissed, but I didn't want to make a scene about it so I just sat there looking stunned. Later that night, she came back out and apologized and I kinda fell for her. I couldn't believe it because I wasn't even out like that, and still am not. I messed around with her for about a year but that whole thing was too much for me." Paul stared into a candle's flame and swirled his glass round and round, reliving that period in his mind.

"What do you mean when you say you're not out like that?" Calvin asked.

"You know, I don't put my lifestyle out there like that," Paul replied.

"What is your lifestyle?" Calvin had no clue what Paul was talking about.

"You're kidding right? How well do you know Lavender? Do you know her real name?" Paul asked with a laughing snort.

"We got to know each other pretty well on the bus, but she never told me any other name. I did think Lavender was an unusual name for a black woman though." Calvin was as confused as ever.

"Lavert. Lavender's birth-given name is Lavert Michael Thompson." Paul watched Calvin's expression anxiously.

"*She's a man?* But she's so ladylike and pretty. And she has breasts." Calvin could not believe it.

"She's been taking pills for years to get those breasts. But trust me, below the waist she *is* a man. When we were together, she only dressed for shows and used pads for breasts. Now, she's a woman round the clock. So now do you know what I mean when I say my lifestyle?" Paul's now red and glassy eyes stared at Calvin sheepishly.

"I think I get it," Calvin said in a low embarrassed tone.

Calvin did not tell Paul about Randolph, nor did he relate what he and Randolph did to this "lifestyle" Paul talked about. In his mind, he and Randolph had just been close enough friends to allow one another to experiment on each other's body. No more, no less.

Chapter 14

Paul discouraged Calvin from even attempting to get a job because it would be an overwhelming feat getting to and from anywhere he worked. The new housing development where Paul lived was quite remote and not on a regular bus route. Calvin was therefore somewhat trapped; however, if he had to be trapped, it was truly nice to be trapped in such a comfortable home. Paul assured Calvin that he would not really need any money. He told him that he would feed, clothe, and take care of all his needs as long as Calvin was under his roof. Although Calvin was skeptical and could not understand why someone would be so generous, he was still sixteen. And at sixteen, such an offer is not questioned much.

Paul had taken Calvin shopping and spent hundreds of dollars buying him the latest fashions. He dressed him up and down in malls and department stores like a child would a dress up doll. "Try it with these shoes…", "Now put on the green shirt…", "You need a black belt with that…", "Now let's look at jeans…" Paul seemed to be having as good of a time as Calvin.

Near the end of July, Calvin called the college and after being transferred and placed on hold many times was told that he needed to get a government issued photo ID prior to registering for any classes. He was also told that he had only a couple of weeks to accomplish this and getting an ID was a tedious chore so he needed to get right on it. When he told Paul his dilemma, Paul told him not to worry and promised he would take care of it.

"But don't I need to go somewhere to apply for an ID right away? What will they need to make me an ID? I don't have a birth certificate," Calvin whined.

"Don't worry Calvin, I have it under control." Paul firmly and confidently quieted Calvin with the one statement.

A few days before registration, Calvin inquired of Paul again what the plan would be to get him in school. Paul rolled his eyes slightly as if annoyed. He had already had a few cocktails that evening and his speech was now a little slurred and the whites of his eyes were pink.

"Calvin, if you ask me about that damn school one more time, you're gonna be on the street. I told you not to worry about it, ok?" Paul said in an annoyed, parental tone. This was not the wonderful Paul Calvin had come to know.

"I understand Paul, but it's just a few days before I'm supposed to register and move in, and I don't have an ID or any of the papers I'm supposed to have." Calvin could feel the panic climbing up his chest into his throat. He refused to allow his eyes to water in front of Paul.

"If you don't get to go this time, there's always next semester, Calvin. Grow up. This is real life; people don't always get what they want when they want it," Paul said as casually as if he was discussing the weather.

Calvin fell silent as his fair skinned cheeks turned white as a ghost. He could not believe his ears. This man spoke of his dream, the only thing that had been keeping him going, as if it were some last minute idea. *"There's always next semester?"* It dawned on Calvin that Paul had no intention of helping him get in school if it meant him leaving his house. He enjoyed having Calvin there, but Calvin could not figure out why. That same night, he got his answer.

Although Calvin had gone to bed early, it took him hours of tossing and turning before he actually got to sleep. His stomach churned in cramps and his chest felt the uncomfortable pressure of stress and worry. It was a hot night and he slept atop the thick comforter in his boxers alone.

Calvin began to dream an erotic dream of Randolph exploring his body as he had before. He could feel Randolph's tongue licking the tip of his dick. He could feel Randolph's lips wrap themselves around his now hard dick and begin to suck it. This time, Randolph was not as gentle as he had been in times past. He sucked with much more vigor and hunger. Calvin twisted and groaned in as much discomfort as pleasure. He felt hands holding his waist still as he was being sucked. Randolph's hands now seemed smaller than before. Calvin had not thought about sexual pleasure since he had been in Atlanta and this dream was a welcome release. As Randolph sucked Calvin ferociously in the dream, Calvin let himself enjoy it, his dick jumping against the roof of Randolph's mouth. After a very few minutes, Calvin could take the pleasure no more and let himself go. His chest rose and his leg muscles tightened. His whole body convulsed as a volcano erupted. The climax seemed to go on for minutes as the hot liquid shot over and over out of his dick.

As the climax shook him awake, he felt the hot sting strike his face. He had been slapped hard on his cheek.

"Don't you ever cum in my mouth again, bitch!" Paul exclaimed after spitting into the cocktail glass he had apparently brought in with him as he came in to molest Calvin in his sleep.

Paul rolled his naked body off Calvin's bed and stumbled out as if nothing had happened. Calvin's mind took him back to that terrible night in another lifetime when Vernon had entered his room in the middle of the night and taken the first piece of his innocence away. As he lay in his now defiled bed still feeling the vibrating sting on his face, he wondered why these things happened to him? What was he doing to invite these men to touch him?

Was he now doomed to just go with it? If he showed disapproval of Paul's actions, where would he live now that he had no hope of going to college this semester? Once again, Calvin was trapped by circumstances he felt he had no control over.

The next morning, a Sunday morning, Calvin woke to the smell of a home cooked breakfast. His mind took him a million miles away back to Gran's kitchen in Woolfe, but more modern and sophisticated than that. He could smell the greasy smell of bacon, the fruitful baked aroma of blueberry muffins, and a flavored coffee brewing. Reluctantly, he entered the bright kitchen, which was quite alive this morning. The shades were wide open and the sunlight hit the black and white tile lighting up the whole kitchen like an operating room. The strong gospel voice of James Cleveland was blasting for the Lord to "Do It". Paul was crooning along as he hustled around the kitchen putting out the colorful dishes he liked to use for breakfast.

"Oh hey! Come on in and sit down. I thought it would be nice to have a good Sunday breakfast today. I'm going to church later if you want to go with me, but you'll have to hurry, it starts at eleven," Paul said cheerfully.

For a brief moment, Calvin wondered if the events of last night were all a dream. The wonderful dream about Randolph embedded in a nightmare about Paul. Then he touched his face and felt the slight soreness of the wild slap and knew it was real. Neither Paul nor Calvin ever mentioned that night and life went on as usual for a few weeks.

As the leaves on the trees around Paul's house began to turn shades of orange, brown, and red, Calvin began having feelings of nostalgia. He could hear Gran humming *Amazing Grace* as she hung clothes out on the line behind the house. He could smell the buttery aroma of baked chicken and dumplings in the oven. He mostly missed being in school. He loved the idea of learning and growing. When he was in school, he felt like he was moving toward some exciting, prosperous end. Now, as he just sat around watching TV everyday, he felt totally useless, idle, and trapped.

"Do you think I could ride to work with you and look for a job in the city?" Calvin asked Paul one evening as they ate the country dinner of fried chicken, homemade macaroni and cheese, collard greens and corn bread that Calvin had prepared.

"Even if you got one, you know it would be too complicated for you to get there on the bus from here," Paul objected.

"Well, maybe I could find a job near yours and ride to and from work with you," Calvin said hopefully.

"Listen, I have a pretty free schedule on my job. I go and come as I please. I don't want to be put on a schedule because you have to be at work at a particular time. And I don't want to have to stay late waiting for you if I decide to leave work early. Calvin, you do not need a job. Don't you have a roof over your head? Don't you have plenty of food to eat? Don't you have more clothes than you could wear? I can take care of all your needs. Don't worry about it," Paul replied and dismissed the conversation.

"You just keep making these dynamite meals like this and you'll be fine. Boy, you cook like my grandmother used to cook. But I want you to learn some contemporary dishes too, not just country food," Paul added.

"Sure," Calvin responded, disappointed that he would not be allowed to get a job.

Chapter 15

Calvin wrapped himself in his cooking. He would watch every cooking show he could find on television looking for new dishes to try. When Paul would take him shopping, Calvin always asked to go to a bookstore and buy a new cookbook, which Paul readily agreed to, knowing he would reap the benefits of a great meal. Calvin had the gift of cooking any dish he attempted to perfection. He also loved for his dishes to have exquisite presentation. Even his meatloaf would be garnished with colorful pepper slices arranged to look like daisies atop the loaf. Every day that Paul came home, he walked in to a wonderful new aroma and he loved it.

For the first couple of months that Calvin lived with Paul, no one ever visited. Paul placed and received several phone calls where he would laugh and talk for hours on end, but no one actually came to the house. After a couple of months, Paul began going out on weekend evenings, telling Calvin to keep the doors locked and not to wait up for him. Now Paul's social life had seemingly escalated and he was going out more frequently and coming home drunk, often not alone.

Thanksgiving rolled around and Calvin began to feel depressed as he reminisced about last year's Thanksgiving and that faithful night before when Randolph had taken him on a sexual trip out of his mind. He managed to busy himself and focus his thoughts on cooking a wonderful traditional Thanksgiving dinner for Paul and a couple of his friends who apparently had no family in Atlanta.

The formal dining room was exquisite. Paul had gone out and purchased fall colored accessories for the season. A tan tablecloth covered the table with a leaf patterned orange runner. Orange and tan tapered candles in wooden candleholders adorned the setting. Calvin had set out Paul's fine china dishes and real silverware. A huge cornucopia filled with fresh fall flowers crowned the table. It was a setting to be photographed for a magazine.

The food was unbelievable. Calvin had been working half the night and all morning preparing turkey, dressing, vegetables, pies, cakes, and any number of delicacies. Each dish was artfully arranged and garnished on its dish. Calvin was very proud of his meal and stood smiling and admiring its beauty and wonderful aroma before serving it.

"Wow, this is so pretty that I hate to eat it," Kenny, one of the guests, said in amazement once he entered the laid out dining room.

"Thank you," Calvin bashfully responded to the man he had just met.

"Yeah, you need to come cook for me sometimes. I'll pay you," David said jokingly.

Suddenly Calvin was feeling very proud and loosened up. "Paul is not going to let me do anything for anyone else. He won't even let me have a job," Calvin laughed as he joked back with David.

Paul immediately shot Calvin a serious look then laughed along almost nervously.

The day was long and filled with a lot of preparation then clean up for Calvin, but it was worth it all to him for the feeling for accomplishment and pride he got from preparing that wonderful meal and seeing how much the other men enjoyed it. He hadn't felt this much pride and self worth since his graduation night.

Paul and his friends had wine with dinner, beer as they watched the Thanksgiving bowl games on TV, and graduated to cocktails in the evening. Paul seemed to drink more than the other two men together. Consequently, by the night's end, Paul had transformed into the red-eyed, angry man Calvin hated and slightly feared.

When Calvin had finally finished putting away the leftover food and cleaning all the dishes, he went into his room thoroughly exhausted. Just as he had stripped down to his briefs, the bedroom door violently burst open and hit the wall behind it. Paul stood for a brief moment in the doorframe, eyes red and full of fury. He rushed Calvin and drew back his left hand, balled his fist and threw a punch packed with the force of steel into Calvin's face. Calvin staggered into the dresser knocking over all the expensive colognes Paul had bought him.

"What the *fuck* do you mean trying to make my friends think I'm holding you hostage here or something? *'Paul won't even let me work'*... Don't you know saying some shit like that could ruin my name? You just turned seventeen. What if that got back to my job or my church? I should put your ass out on the street to fend for yourself since you don't know how to appreciate what I do for you."

Calvin stood motionless in fear as blood flowed from his nose. He knew he could fight back and probably overtake Paul, but then what? Where would he go? Then Calvin questioned in his mind, *"Did I bring this on myself? I shouldn't have said that to David. I wouldn't want to cause Paul's reputation to be tarnished."*

"I'm sorry Paul. I won't say anything like that again." Calvin said with both tears and blood washing his face.

"Go take care of that blood. And don't let anybody hit you in your face again. I don't want that pretty face scared. Understand me?" Paul said, now calm.

"I understand," Calvin answered but Paul had turned and began walking away.

Hours later, Calvin was awakened by the stream of light from the hallway as his bedroom door squeaked open. He looked over at the high-tech digital clock radio on the nightstand to see it flash 3:07 a.m. Remembering the last visit from Paul, he lay perfectly still with his eyes closed tight in an effort to feign sleep. Paul took a seat on the side of the bed and began to caress Calvin's bare back.

"Calvin, baby I just wanted to check on you to make sure you were o.k. You seemed pretty upset earlier," Paul whispered as if there was anyone else in the house to be awakened by his voice.

"Make sure *I* am o.k.? *I* seemed upset? *You* are the one who hauled off and hit me," Calvin thought but dared not speak aloud. Calvin's nose began to throb mildly at the memory of the strike it had taken earlier.

"Calvin, I know you can hear me. I just want you to know that I get so passionate about these things because I care about you and I don't want you to have to leave because of some gossip about our life together here. I truly hate when you make me lose my temper. Calvin, I want you to know... I love you," Paul softly explained to Calvin's turned head.

Although his head was turned and Paul couldn't see them, Calvin's eyes were now wide open and beginning to fill with tears. He could not recall any man, or woman, saying those words to him before. "I love you," three little words with so much power. Having never really heard the words, Calvin was caught totally off guard at the effect they could have. Those words could reach down into a man's chest, thump a stopped heart, and cause it to beat again. Those words could take the blinders off a man's eyes and cause him to see the true beauty in a world he thought was all gloom. Calvin longed for those words from his father, his mother, Gran, his siblings, Zelda, and even Randolph; but none of those people had come through. Now, in the middle of the night, the man who a minute ago was his captor had instantly become the one to set him free.

Calvin flipped over and allowed Paul to look into his teary brown eyes for a moment before Calvin lifted his head and kissed Paul's lips. Calvin was feeling more appreciation than love, but his tender age and innocence had not taught him the difference.

Paul took the cue and immediately began kissing Calvin ferociously. Calvin was a little taken aback, remembering the sensual, passionate kisses he had received from Randolph. Paul was much more aggressive. He sucked and bit Calvin's thick lower lip after licking his whole face like a too playful dog. Paul managed to break for a moment to flip his white tee shirt over his head and onto the floor. Calvin's chest was already bare. Paul climbed atop Calvin and nibbled and licked his face, ears, neck and chest like a starving animal. He all of a sudden, pecked a kiss on Calvin's lips and quickly rose from the bed and walked out of the room leaving the door ajar. Before Calvin could get up and close the door, Paul returned without his underwear on as before. Calvin saw the silhouette of his small dick standing straight out as he entered the dark bedroom. Paul re-joined Calvin on the bed and without warning took Calvin's jockey underwear off and flung them across the floor. He wrapped his right hand around Calvin's deflated but still fat penis and began slapping himself in the face with it, sighing heavily with lots of "oue's and ah's" before taking it into his mouth. As Calvin felt the warm moisture of Paul's mouth engulf him, he began to stiffen and grow to it's fullest potential which was more than Paul could possibly handle in his mouth at once. Paul released Calvin from his mouth and hoisted himself into a squatting position above Calvin's waist. He took Calvin's hard dick in his hand and began forcing it into himself. He had apparently applied a lubricating substance in and around his hole, which caused Calvin to slide right into him.

"Oh damn!" Paul cried out as he lowered himself onto Calvin's dick for the first time.

Paul began to bounce up and down on Calvin much like Calvin remembered playing on Gran's worn out mattress as a child. With each bounce Paul would grunt a little louder, go further onto Calvin, and began to bounce faster. Calvin had never felt the pleasure of being ridden before, and although it was a little awkward for him, he did like the way it felt as it moved him closer and closer to a climax.

Paul could tell Calvin was coming close to an end and could feel his dick throbbing inside him.

"Go ahead, let it go. I want to feel it," Paul instructed Calvin.

On cue, Calvin's leg muscles tightened, toes curled and his face contorted like a weightlifter's. His body visibly shook as he squirted his liquid into Paul. Instantly, Paul shot his onto Calvin's chest with much more dramatic expression.

"Shit!" Paul screamed out, collapsing off of Calvin and onto the bed.

"Well, get cleaned up and get some sleep," Paul said after catching his breath.

He hopped up and left the room as if he and Calvin had just watched the news on TV and now were going to bed. All of Paul's affection for Calvin had apparently been dispensed and was now running down Calvin's chest as he sat up on his elbows watching Paul exit without so much as a, "good night." Calvin lay back, listening to the faint sound of the shower running in Paul's master bathroom down the hall.

Chapter 16

Sexual activity between Paul and Calvin continued on a regular basis but was never the passionate love making Calvin longed for. Calvin always felt slightly molested after Paul left his room. Sex with Paul was rough, quick, animalistic, and dirty; unlike the wonderful experiences he had with Randolph in a time that seemed to be decades ago. Paul would always come to Calvin late at night, and leave as quickly as he had come. He only kissed Calvin when he had been drinking, licking his alcohol-soaked tongue all over Calvin's face in a drunken effort to find the right spot. Calvin often cringed when he would hear his door opening in the night, but he felt that allowing Paul to gratify himself was his only way of paying him for his generosity and alleged "love", something Calvin so desperately desired.

One night when Calvin noticed that Paul was drinking his usual fill, he thought maybe locking his door would present an obstacle and cause Paul to leave him alone this one time. Big mistake. Calvin awakened to a loud thud at the door.

"Open this damn door!" Paul shouted from the other side.

Calvin lay still for a moment, weighing the best course of action. Then, after a second thud that sounded like Paul's open palm hitting the door with all his force, Calvin leaped out of his bed and twisted the round knob to release the lock... click. Immediately after the door was unlocked it swung open startlingly fast almost hitting Calvin. Like a flash, Paul was in the room slightly swaying, fighting for balance. Calvin reached out to help him stand. Without any warning, Paul backhanded Calvin with brut force. The force and sting of the slap was so great it knocked Calvin off his feet as big as he was.

"Don't you ever lock a door in this house to keep me out. Who the fuck do you think you are? This is *my* house and the only reason you are here is because I let you live here," Paul snorted.

Still slightly dizzy from the slap and fall, Calvin could hear a distant ringing in his head. He collected himself and climbed onto the bed. The Jekyll and Hyde routine was on again, Paul rushed to his side like a worried parent.

"Are you o.k. Baby? I hate seeing you in pain. Why do you make me hit you like that? You're so beautiful, don't you know I don't want you all scared up?" Paul's performance seemed almost believable.

He caressed Calvin's genitals first gently and then with more vigor when he detected no response from Calvin's large floppy appendage. Normally Calvin's dick would stiffen at the mildest touch, but not tonight, and this began to upset Paul because he wanted it so badly. He put his hand in Calvin's underwear and began to fondle his softness.

"Please don't. Not tonight," Calvin pleaded.

"Fuck you, you yellow bitch!" Paul snorted at Calvin through clenched teeth as he rose from the bed and left the room. He slammed the door so hard that the small framed print of a sandy beach hanging on the wall fell off as a result of the vibration. Calvin knew then that he would pay for his refusal.

The next few days were brutal. Paul barely spoke to Calvin. Calvin cooked all his favorite meals each day, which Paul ate in silence, usually while watching TV in the living room, not at the dinner table, as was their custom. Whenever Calvin tried to start a conversation with Paul, he would walk out of the room or get on the telephone with one of his mystery friends. Calvin began to be afraid that Paul was planning to put him out.

After a whole week of this treatment, the weekend rolled around again. Paul slept in Saturday morning, rising just before noon. When he finally came out of his room, he was fully dressed, grabbing his keys and heading out the door without a word. Calvin's stomach twisted in nervousness as he sat and watched this deliberate display of hostility.

Paul always told Calvin when he would be home or he would tell him not to wait up because it would be very late. This time, Calvin had no idea when Paul would return and he began to worry a little when he hadn't heard from him by midnight. Though he lay in his bed, he did not sleep. His eyes opened every time a car passed the house, thinking it may be Paul.

Finally as the red digital numbers displayed 2:47 a.m., he heard the remote chain mechanism pulling the garage door open. This sound eased his mind as he was concerned for Paul's safety; at the same time it worried him that Paul would be drunk and feeling like confrontation or worse, some rough variation of sex. Then to his surprise, he heard two car doors shut.

There was loud talking in the hallway for a moment, which Calvin was unable to discern before Paul's door slammed closed as if Paul wanted to be sure Calvin was awakened even if he were asleep. Nonetheless, Calvin rested easier knowing that Paul was home safe entertaining company and therefore would not bother him. He did not know how wrong he was.

Not long after he had drifted off to sleep, Calvin was awakened by the weight of a strong muscular man gliding over him, allowing his heaviness to press onto him as he lay half sleep on his back. Before he opened his eyes, he knew it was not Paul. This man was very muscular and solid. The man had pulled the covers back and was grinding his nude body back and forth against Calvin's. Although he was confused and a little startled, this felt very good to Calvin. Calvin could feel that the man had a large dick and it was hard rubbing against his now hard dick still protected by underwear. Calvin could feel that the man had put some lubricant on his dick. The man smelled of underarm odor, alcohol, and cheap cologne and his chest was wet in perspiration. As he gripped his hands around the band of Calvin's underwear and started to pull them down, Calvin grabbed his hands and stopped him.

"Who are you?" Calvin asked in a breathy whisper.

The man did not answer, nor did he like Calvin stopping him. He yanked the underwear from Calvin's grip and pulled them down to his knees and pushed them the rest of the way off with his feet, glaring into Calvin's eyes the whole time. Without saying one word from his mouth, Calvin knew that this man's eyes said, "I will hurt you if I have to." Although Calvin had been doing hundreds of push-ups each day and was in fantastic tone and shape, he was no match for this anonymous brut.

The man grabbed Calvin's ankles and lifted his legs in the air against the force of Calvin's resistance, saddling them on his own shoulders. He leaned his strong body down onto Calvin forcing Calvin to fold over as if he were an overstuffed suitcase. Calvin was clamped in with little maneuverability when he felt the man's big dick pushing its moist, lubricated head into him. Calvin grunted then cried out, "No! Stop! Please don't do this! Paauul!!!"

"Don't call me. You don't want to fuck me anymore, so I got somebody to fuck me *and you* real good. This nigga got a dick bigger than yours!" Paul said with a laugh.

Calvin couldn't believe it. Paul had been in the room the whole time watching this man rape him.

As the man went faster and faster, deeper and deeper into Calvin, Paul stepped up out of the shadows masturbating himself in pleasure at the sight of Calvin crying in pain, shame and disappointment. "Yeah, fuck him good nigga. That's why I'm paying you top dollar. Give him all eleven inches. He think he the only nigga with a big dick," Paul sneered.

Chapter 17

"Get dressed. Wear something nice, I need you to go to a funeral with me today." Paul spat out the order as calmly as if he'd asked for a glass of water.

It was Saturday morning, the day after Calvin's twenty-fifth birthday. Calvin had long ago given up the idea of actually celebrating birthdays ever since Paul actually beat him with a belt on the night of his eighteenth birthday because the attractive waiter at the restaurant Paul had taken him to had flirted shamelessly with him in Paul's presence. Paul accused Calvin of flirting back and first slapped him, then made him strip down to his beautifully toned nude body before beating him like a bad child with his belt. Since that year's tragic celebration, Calvin quietly made himself a special birthday meal and celebrated in his own mind, never mentioning it to anyone else. Without fail, a couple of weeks later Paul would say, "Isn't your birthday around this time?"

"Who died?" Calvin asked curiously.

Calvin assumed it was another of the older members of the Church were Paul was very involved. Over the years, Paul's involvement in church had escalated exponentially from a guy who visits twice a month. When Paul first took Calvin to church with him, they sat together. Over time, Calvin was instructed where to sit while Paul made his seat on the front row of the choir singing a loud and high tenor. Later, Calvin sat in the back as Paul began to sit on the front row serving with the other church trustees and deacons. Finally, Calvin was totally knocked off his feet when one Sunday after Paul had not taken with him to church for a few weeks, Calvin was sitting in the back and noticed Paul stepping up to the fiberglass pulpit podium after being introduced as *Minister* Paul Hopkins to lead the congregation in prayer.

"*Minister*? This minister, the guy on the organ, and one of the guys in the tenor section just fucked me and each other Friday night," Calvin thought in fury at the idea of playing with God. First there was Gran quoting scriptures and teaching women how to live "holy", but failing to follow the most basic Christian principle of loving her own grandson. Now, here was a man who was a virtual alcoholic with fetishes for the sickest sexual acts, which included watching the repeated brutal rape of the person he claimed to love by dozens of men, sometimes three or four in one session. Here was this man, praying to the Almighty God on behalf of over a thousand unknowing, innocent people. The thought made Calvin so angry that he marched out as the organist chimed in to back Paul's emotional performance and stir the crowd to a frenzy. Despite the white-gloved usher's attempt to stop him from walking during prayer, Calvin pushed the sanctuary door so vigorously that it swung back and forth a few times before settling. Paul did not lose momentum, as Calvin could hear the music escalating to a lively church dance beat and parishioners shouting their approval.

"A friend of mine. I just think you should go with me to this funeral. O.k.? No more questions. Dress nice, there will be a lot of people there and this time I want you to sit with me." Calvin knew by Paul's quick response that he did not want to discuss this any further.

Now Calvin was totally confused. Paul would never let him sit with him at church for fear that someone may make out the connection between them; whatever that connection is. After all these years, there was still no official definition to Calvin and Paul's relationship. They were not just friends, if friends at all. Although Paul was careful to shelter Calvin from as much of the real free world as possible, Calvin had seen other gay couples and knew that he and Paul were not a couple. They also were not family. Calvin loved Paul because Paul was all he knew or had so he was forced to focus all his affection on him.

The funeral was at Thompson Brothers Memorial Chapel funeral home. Calvin was surprised it was not held at a church. As much as he already hated funerals and honestly was a little spooked by them, he really did not want to go inside a funeral home.

The funeral was at 2:00 p.m., and it was 1:57 as Paul zipped his new Mercedes into an open parking space in front of the old brick building on Atlanta's West End. As Paul rushed Calvin through the entrance, there was a line of people snaking their way into the surprisingly large chapel, already full except for a few seats sprinkled here and there. Apparently, Thompson Brothers had decided instead of having several small chapels for funerals, to invest all its available space into one large chapel that could be divided into smaller ones when the need arose or used as one for services like this one. The funeral director at the chapel door whispered to Paul and Calvin that they were out of programs for now and to catch onto the tail end of the line for viewing before the service begins.

"We're not going to open her up anymore after this. But she wanted to make sure people saw how beautiful she would look laid out. She made all these arrangements herself; wrote her own program and paid it all in cash." The chatty little old man in white gloves hissed out.

"Old queen," Paul muttered and slightly shook his head as he and Calvin stepped away from the funeral director, now pleased with himself for giving all the "tea" he could in the small amount of time he had.

"I'll wait here," Calvin said, suddenly realizing he had no memory of ever seeing a dead person. He had been too young to remember his father's funeral, and Gran never made the children go to the funerals of church members and family in Woolfe.

"No, come with me," Paul insisted and without waiting for argument, caught up with the viewing line.

Calvin walked beside Paul but slightly behind him. He wore black slacks, a black suede jacket and black turtleneck. Paul, dressed in a charcoal tailored suit, had looked him over approvingly before stepping out of the house. He did look as fine as fifty year old wine swaggering along nervously down the aisle, unaware that more than half the seated assembly had mournful yet hungry eyes on him.

As they came closer to the casket, the sniffles around them became sobs, and sobs became wails. Calvin could literally hear his heart beating as he drew closer and closer to the neat gray metal box amidst the sea of gaudy floral arrangements. Some of the flowers were gracefully unassuming and appropriate. Others were tacky and childlike. One displayed a toy telephone surrounded by "GOD CALLED YOU HOME" spelled in tiny multicolored carnations...tacky. The three minutes it took to reach the casket seemed to take three hours in Calvin's imagination.

For all his nervousness, Calvin could not have been prepared for what literally lay ahead. As he reached the casket, Calvin kept his eyes focused on Paul. He did not want to look at the dead body of this stranger. However, the sparkling shimmer in the casket caught in the line of his eyesight and his curiosity was pulled to look. There she lay, as radiant as a bride on her wedding day; as regal as a queen on her throne, as helpless as Calvin himself felt. There lay a thinner, darker Lavender Chiffon. She wore a lavender sequined evening gown that sparkled like a clear summer night's sky.

Calvin froze in his footsteps... in horror.

"Why didn't you tell me!" Calvin spoke aloud causing the trio in the corner of the chapel singing some ballad about seeing her again to stop mid verse.

"Shut up and come on! You're making a fool of yourself," Paul whispered between clinched teeth and pulled Calvin along.

Paul located a couple of seats near the back and instructed Calvin to sit. For the duration of the service, Calvin stared blankly ahead, comprehending only in small pieces anything going on around him. He felt like he had been lifted above the world and now looked down on it, removed of its activities. One man who could barely compose himself enough to speak explained that he was about to read the eulogy Lavender had written for herself a few days ago when she knew she would not make it much longer. As Calvin still floated about the world in his mind, he could hear the man read, *"Baby, I lived life. I found a way to live my dreams whether people liked it or not. I did not leave unfulfilled. I loved and was loved which is the most important thing in life. Baby, listen to Miss Lavender, do whatever it takes to experience true love at least once. Settle for nothing less."*

Calvin knew then what he had to do... and he dreaded it.

Chapter 18

As Calvin walked sluggishly behind Paul to the car after the brief but beautiful service, Calvin was awakened from his daze by his name.

"Calvin?"

Calvin turned to find a slightly thicker, more attractive Darnell grinning from ear to ear standing behind him.

"Darnell? Hey man!" Calvin was thrilled to see anyone from a life other than the imprisonment he had been experiencing with Paul for nearly nine years.

"Calvin. We have to go." Paul's command was firm and final.

"Give me your number and I'll call you man," Calvin said apologetically.

"Sure. Here, take my card. I finished school and have a real job with business cards and all now. My pager number is at the bottom," Darnell said with a chuckle.

"Calvin! Let's go!" The shout came from a now visibly angry Paul.

Calvin slid the card into his pocket before turning around hoping Paul did not notice him taking it. He realized there would be trouble about this encounter with Darnell anyway, but he did not want to lose the chance to have someone from the outside world to talk to.

By the time Calvin reached the sleek black Mercedes, Paul had already put the car in drive and was releasing his foot from the brake a little so that the car rolled a little as Calvin closed the door.

The ride home was so tense and long, they could have easily taken a road trip across country to California in seemingly less time. Neither Paul nor Calvin uttered one word the entire way. Paul did not turn on the radio as he usually did immediately when he started the car. Not even the sounds from the expressway penetrated the car. For the first time, Calvin regretted the luxury of a soundproof interior that this new Mercedes provided.

Calvin was still stunned at the fact that Paul would take him to Lavender's funeral without ever telling him she, or he, was dead. Then there was the startling realization that this terrible virus he heard so much about on television was real. Calvin now had to face the reality that people are indeed dying from AIDS. Until this point, it was just something he heard Paul and his friends talk about as they discussed the declining health or death of remote people he had never met or cared about. Whenever Paul spoke of someone he knew having AIDS, he softened the painful reality of it by referring to the person as having "the package", or being "sick". No longer did sick ever mean a cold, stomach virus, or even cancer. Those illnesses now had to be referred to by their individual and proper names. "Sick" had a deeper, more fatal inference.

When the car was safely parked in it's space in the garage, Paul turned the ignition off, released himself from the restraint of the seatbelt, and without thought or hesitation slapped Calvin so hard that his head snapped against the passenger window.

"Don't you ever disrespect me like that again," Paul hissed through his trademark clenched teeth.

Calvin could feel a thousand prickles of pain on the left side of his face. The slap came as a total surprise to him and he still was processing what just happened. This day had been full of surprises.

After a couple of minutes of silence and looking straight ahead at the garage wall, Paul turned to Calvin with a look of near disgust and asked, "Who was that faggot that had you all up in his face grinning like you was in love with him? Don't lie to me, I could tell that you two have been fucking."

"That was Darnell, the guy from the hotel I stayed at before I moved here. I have never done anything with him." Calvin was about to cry; then for the first time, held back his tears and decided he would no longer just take it.

"If you want to talk about disrespect, let's talk about taking me to that funeral and not telling me that it was the funeral of the person who was there for me when I was at my lowest state. Do you know what a shock that was? I will never forget the horror of seeing Lavender like that." Calvin spoke calmly but without the fear that Paul was used to hearing in his voice.

Paul did not respond to Calvin's statement. He simply got out of the car and went into the house. Calvin decided to sit in the parked car for a few minutes before following him inside. Neither Darnell nor the funeral was spoken of again. As a matter of fact, there wasn't much conversation at all for the rest of the weekend outside of necessary questions and answers.

Monday morning finally rolled around and Calvin lay anxiously in bed waiting for Paul to finally leave the house. He had to exercise all his self-control not to jump out of the bed as soon as he heard the door leading to the garage close. He wanted to be sure Paul wouldn't come back in for a forgotten item or decide to fix a snack while the car warmed. Once he heard the delightful sound of the garage door opening and finally closing, he jumped out of the bed and headed for the kitchen to grab the new cordless phone.

Calvin went to the closet, reached inside the pocket of his black suede jacket and retrieved the deep blue business card. In silver foil Helvetica read, "AHE Commercial Designs". The line beneath read, "Darnell E. Jacobs, Architect". Calvin was astonished. For some reason, he could not picture Darnell as anything other than a struggling young man working late nights at a low rated motel. He dialed the number listed as his pager number, input his number when prompted, and hung up.

"Well, that's that." He spoke aloud to himself with a sigh as he returned the phone to its base. He immediately regretted the page, not knowing what he would say when or if Darnell called back.

Five minutes later, the phone rang.

"Did someone page Darnell Jacobs?" Darnell spoke in an official, professional voice that Calvin barely recognized.

"Uh... yes, this is Calvin, Calvin Sharpe." Calvin hesitantly identified himself. He had no clue where this conversation would go from here. He immediately felt a strange embarrassment for having paged Darnell disturbing him from important work.

"If this is a bad time, I can page you again when it's more convenient," Calvin apologized.

"No! Man, I was hoping you would get in touch with me soon. I thought all weekend about how good it was to see you. So how have you been? Man, I thought you had dropped off the face of the earth." Darnell reassured Calvin.

"I've been o.k. man, there isn't too much happening with me," Calvin replied, happy that Darnell seemed to be enthusiastic about the conversation.

"Calvin, I know we never talked about this kind of stuff when you were at the hotel all those years ago, so it's a little awkward now. But, was that man you were with your lover?" Darnell asked.

After a few seconds of silence Calvin responded, "I don't really know."

"What do you mean, you don't know? Either you are together or not," Darnell said with a slight chuckle.

"Darnell, I was so glad to see you because I really need to talk to someone. I know we haven't talked in over eight years, but I remember what a caring person you are. I know I can trust you."

"Of course you can. I knew you were not happy when I saw you. At first, I thought it was just the sadness of being at a funeral, but the more I thought about it, I knew that there was a deeper misery there than that," Darnell said with obvious compassion in his voice.

"I am miserable, Darnell. I have been miserable for a long time, too long. You know, I don't think I've ever really been happy here. I need to leave this house Darnell," Calvin admitted aloud for the first time ever.

"You need to get out? Well let's meet for lunch or something," Darnell replied with innocent ignorance of Calvin's meaning.

"No Darnell, I need to leave here for good. I can't tell you some of the things I go through here. I am twenty-five years old and I haven't had a job since I was sixteen. I don't leave this house but once or twice a week, and then only under *his* supervision. When I go to church, I have to be sure to look straight ahead the entire time because if he sees me from the *pulpit* looking in the general direction of any man, I will suffer the consequences when we get home. Darnell, the reason you never heard from me after I left the hotel is he doesn't allow me to have friends or communicate with anyone in the outside world. I could have been a great doctor by now, but he wouldn't let me go to school. He finds petty reasons to beat up on me at least once a month. To answer your question, no we are not lovers. It took Lavender to give me a message that even death couldn't conceal. I am determined to experience true love at least once, and this isn't it." Calvin stopped short of his next statement realizing he was ranting. But he felt good and strong. This was the first time he had ever identified or verbalized these feelings.

"Oh Calvin, I had no idea man. Why have you gone through this for so long? You're bigger than him. Why do you let him beat you? Man, I'm so sorry. I wish I had known way back then that you were even gay. I would have never let you go off with some strange older man to God knows where."

"I don't know why I let him hit me and treat me like this. I guess I thought I loved him or that he loved me. I was so desperate for love that even brutal love was worth the pain. Do you believe we have never spent one night in the same bedroom?" Calvin said, now giving over to disgusted laughter.

"What? Do you guys have sex?" Darnell asked incredulously.

"Please don't even go there man. You could not begin to believe what's been going on over here." Calvin dreaded this next segment of the conversation. He was afraid Darnell would look down on him for his role in the perverted happenings, but he knew he needed to talk it all out so he continued.

"Darnell, Paul rapes me. And he lets, no instructs, other men to rape me," Calvin said in a matter of fact tone.

"What?!" Darnell could not manage any other response.

"At least once a week, Paul comes in my room in the middle of the night and forces me to have sex with him in one way or the other. At first, I didn't really know what was going on. Man, when I came here I didn't know anyone else had done any of the things with other men that I had experimented with. Then when Paul started messing with me, I just kinda went with it because I was grateful to him for letting me stay here. Later I wanted to stop but he would get angry and threaten me. He became more and more brutal. When I could no longer get hard with him to give him what he wanted, he started finding guys to come do me." Calvin relayed this information as coolly as if he were rattling off a recipe.

"Man, I am too through. Are you serious? Are you saying this Paul invites guys over to have sex with you?"

"No, I'm saying Paul goes out to clubs and brings guys home to fuck me whether I like it or not. Some of them want to do crazy perverted things to me and he makes me let them." Calvin finally began to show some emotion in his voice as he thought about all the men who had violated him, leaving their semen on his back, chest, face, mouth, and worst of all, inside him.

"O.k. that's enough. I'm getting you out of there. I just need to call David first, but I'm sure I can come get you today."

"Who is David?" Calvin asked.

Darnell sighed a short laugh, "Oh, David is my partner... my lover. He would have to be in on a decision like this."

"Darnell, as much as I really want to go, I'm not sure I'm ready to stand up to Paul about this. This man believes he owns me and I think he'll do whatever it takes to keep what is his," Calvin said with a hint of fear. Although he knew he had to make a change, he did not realize it could happen so quickly.

"Calvin, if Paul raped you before you turned seventeen, he could go to prison and he knows that. He is controlling you with fear, the oldest trick in the book. Don't worry about that bastard, you just pack your stuff and be ready to leave *today*. I'll call you back in a few minutes with the plan. Oh, did I tell you David is a Dekalb County Sheriff's deputy? I don't think we're going to have any problems with Paul letting you go." With that, Calvin was reassured.

Chapter 19

Darnell kept his word and called back within minutes to let Calvin know that he and his lover, David, would pick him up at five. This concerned Calvin slightly because that would be right around the time Paul would be getting home. However, the thought that David was a policeman eased Calvin's concern.

Calvin thought his heart would explode through his chest as he nervously watched out the front window for Darnell. It was now fifteen minutes past five and there was no sign of his cavalry. Finally, at 5:20, a gray Jeep Cherokee crept slowly down the street as if the driver was reading the addresses looking for the right house. Calvin felt a ton of stressful worry lift as the Jeep pulled into the drive. A muscular, dark complexioned police officer stepped out of the driver side and Darnell jumped out of the passenger side of the car.

As soon as Calvin opened the ornate front door, Darnell pulled him into a long embrace.

"It's going to be alright now man. We're here to take you away from this madness." Darnell spoke directly into Calvin's ear as he held him.

"Hi, I'm David. Darnell has told me everything and you don't have to worry. This is the start of a new life for you. No one will hurt you again as long as I'm around." Although David did not smile, and probably was the type that seldom smiled, Calvin felt that he was sincere and had a lot of heart. He could see why Darnell had given his heart to this man.

"Let's get your stuff and get the hell out of here," Darnell suggested as he looked around surveying the beautiful home.

Calvin had spent the day packing up all his clothes and intended to leave everything else in his room including the stereo system and television, which were gifts from Paul. Darnell insisted that he strip the room of every last thing he could take. "After eight years of misery, this bastard ought to be moving out and leaving you with the whole house. We're not leaving a damn thing in this room if I can help it. David, help me break down this stereo," Darnell snapped.

Calvin shrugged his shoulders in defeat and began taking his packed boxes of clothes to the door. When he came within ten feet of the front door, he heard the lock turn and the door opened. Within seconds, Paul was inside trying to make sense of what he saw. Calvin froze.

When it became clear what was going on, Paul used his famous clenched-teeth language, "Where the hell do you think you're going and whose car is that in my driveway."

"Paul, I don't want this to be hard. Please let's just let this end peacefully," Calvin pleaded.

"*End* peacefully? Nothing is ending. Whatever you have packed in those boxes belongs to me; you don't own anything. And, you're not going anywhere." Paul moved closer to Calvin reaching to take the two stacked paper boxes from him.

Calvin sat the boxes on floor and did not back down. "Paul, these are my clothes, I'm taking them and I'm leaving."

Paul's eyes narrowed in fury and he drew his right hand back in a stance to backslap Calvin. He stopped his hand in mid-air, registering the scene over Calvin's shoulder.

"Please give me a reason to say you were violent and out of control and I had to shoot you." There was David with his gun drawn and aimed at Paul.

Paul lowered his hand and looked at Calvin incredulously. "You called the police on *me*?"

"No, he called his friend, who happens to be in love with 'the police', you bastard!" Darnell spat out as he revealed himself, stepping out of the hallway laden with stereo speakers.

"Look, I don't know what kind of nonsense Calvin has been telling you guys, but..." Paul started.

"Shut up Paul! This is not nonsense. You will not abuse me any longer. I will leave here and you will never bother me again!" Calvin was determined not to be intimidated by Paul ever again.

"You can leave, you ungrateful bitch! But you are not taking my things anywhere. You will leave just like you came here, with nothing. You may have your little friend with a gun, but I can call the real police and have you picked up for theft." Paul snorted a cruel laugh as he ended his proclamation.

"O.k., if you want to make this a legal matter let's discuss statutory rape from 1982 when Calvin was sixteen. As a matter of fact, let's discuss straight up rape on an ongoing basis throughout Calvin's stay here," Darnell chimed in.

Silence. "I didn't think so. David, Calvin, let's get this shit and get the hell out of this damn house," Darnell said, never losing eye contact with Paul. Paul stood in the same spot by the door as the three of them gathered the things Calvin wanted and walked out the door.

Chapter 20

Darnell and David lived in a very comfortable two-bedroom apartment in Atlanta's illustrious Buckhead community. Buckhead was home to numerous millionaires, as well as a few celebrities. The once "old money" community was now becoming more and more commercialized. Lenox Mall attracted scores of young trendy shoppers while Phipps Plaza appealed to the very high-end shoppers with its outrageously priced designer boutiques.

Calvin moved into the second bedroom in the luxury tower apartment and made a concerted effort to stay out of Darnell and David's way. However, either Darnell or David would constantly call Calvin from his room inviting him to go here and there with them, or come out and meet one of their friends. Calvin eventually felt that both Darnell and David sincerely wanted him there. It was hard for Calvin to warm up and fully appreciate this type of hospitality since Paul's initial welcome had seemingly been just as sincere. Over time, Calvin saw that neither Darnell nor David had any ulterior motive behind his kindness.

On his second week with them, Calvin went against Darnell's advice to just take some time and get used to his freedom. Calvin got dressed in navy slacks, a white shirt, and gold and navy striped tie and took the city bus to Phipp's Plaza and Lenox Mall to fill out job applications immediately after Darnell had left for work. Calvin stood at the bus stop studying the bus line maps to make sure he was taking the right bus. Fortunately, his ride would be pretty quick and easy. He only needed to get on any bus headed north on Peachtree and ride until he saw the Lenox Mall entrance on his right; no transfers, no trains.

When Darnell got home that same evening, there was a delightful surprise waiting for him.

"Oh my God! What have you done here? This is unbelievable. David should be home any minute. He'll love this," Darnell exclaimed as he surveyed the beautiful table Calvin had set.

Calvin had cooked one of his special occasion meals for Darnell and David. There was a huge roast, cooked to perfection and placed on a platter surrounded by potatoes, carrots, and leaves of parsley for décor. There was a basket of rolls, and breads, green bean casserole, a vibrantly colored tossed salad, and on the kitchen counter waiting it's turn to come to the table was a three tiered red velvet cake with cream cheese icing and the words "Thank You" written in red icing. Just as impressive as the food was the table arrangement with candles from all over the house in every free spot Calvin could find on or around the table. The effect was not gaudy, but elegant.

"I hope you don't mind me cooking your food, but I plan to fill the kitchen with groceries when I get my first check," Calvin said grinning.

"First check?" Darnell asked in a playfully knowing tone.

"I'm sorry, I just couldn't stay here and not work and contribute something. I went out today and got a job," Calvin said sheepishly.

"You got a job in one day? Most people look unsuccessfully for jobs for weeks. What will you be doing?"

"I'm going to be a men's department salesman in Macy's at the mall. Since I haven't had a job in nine years and I don't have a college education, it's a pretty good job. I honestly don't know what the guy saw in me. He almost gave me the job before I could finish the application," Calvin explained with a chuckle.

"Was this guy a black man?" Darnell asked.

"Yeah," Calvin answered.

"How old did he seem?"

"I don't know, probably about 30."

"What was he wearing?"

"Some tight black pants and a fitted black sweater. He was really well built, his chest was bulging through the sweater."

"Ha! That's it. He's gay. Sure enough, he made a good decision to hire you because you will be great at anything you do, but he hired you because you look like that. You worked it boy!" Darnell said laughing.

"What are you talking about? Worked what?" Calvin asked, genuinely confused.

"Calvin, please tell me you know that you are drop dead gorgeous. I know that damn Paul took your self esteem away, but please don't tell me he took your self *awareness* away too."

Calvin just looked at Darnell awkwardly for a moment. Before he could respond, the sound of David's rattling keys at the door saved him.

The meal was like none Darnell or David had enjoyed at home before.

"Man, how in the world did you cook all this food *and* get a job in one day?" David asked as a he patted his belly in delightful fullness. The three of them sat around the glass oblong table after consuming the delicious dinner.

"This was a simple meal. One day I'll really do a nice dinner for you guys," Calvin said. He wasn't bragging, but he was genuinely proud of the one thing he knew he did well.

"Calvin, I'm really happy about you getting a job. I know you'll do well at it, but don't settle for selling clothes in Macy's. That's not your final destination. You are a very smart and talented man and you have a bright future. I don't want you to think you have missed your chance at living the life you really wanted," Darnell advised.

Chapter 21

I n a short period of time, Calvin grew to dread his job. He was moved from Young Men's to Men's to Men's Fragrances back to Men's. Although he was one of the popular store's top salesmen, he constantly felt that he was operating beneath his skill level, potential, and destiny. It was not as miserable as his years with Paul, it was not even the same kind of misery as he had experienced in those years, but it was a boring, stagnate kind of misery.

One positive thing that came from Calvin's working in the public eye was that he learned Darnell was not exaggerating about his attractiveness. Calvin had grown up resenting his looks, later finding that people found him attractive, and then through psychological conditioning from Paul found himself to be unattractive and unwanted again. Calvin now garnered stares, winks, tickling handshakes, notes with phone numbers, and flirtatious phone calls at work from recent patrons on a daily basis; some women and most men. Calvin could not believe the attention his humble presence commanded. Even the most modest personality soon takes on an air of confidence in the face of so much attention.

Although many of these men were attractive to Calvin and his mind filled with sexual fantasies about them, only once did a customer leave a lasting impression.

"Excuse me, do you work here?"

The honey colored young man couldn't have been older than twenty but he had an air of maturity and confidence that was very attractive. He was tall and thin, but toned not skinny; and his eyes gleamed like crystal.

"Yes I... Yes I do." Calvin stuttered as he turned around from his labored attempt to fold a stack of shirts on a display table. Calvin was caught off guard by the man behind this voice. Although he wasn't gorgeous in the model kind of way, he had a beauty that was breathtaking to Calvin.

"Uh, where is your cologne for men?" The young man asked. He obviously was as startled by Calvin's beauty as Calvin was by his.

"Men's Fragrances. Straight ahead and to the right," Calvin said looking directly into the man's eyes.

"Thanks," the young customer said and stood a little too long before turning to find the cologne counter.

"Try the new Calvin Klein Escape," Calvin shouted behind him a little too late.

As the young man walked away and Calvin resumed his folding, Calvin turned to get one last glimpse of him. At that same moment, the man turned and caught Calvin's eyes. He gave a slight smile then turned nervously and disappeared into the crowd.

Calvin kicked himself in his mind for several days for not finding a way to get to know that man.

"Why didn't I offer to walk him to the cologne counter and then offer my advice on fragrances? Why didn't I give him my name and tell him I used to work in fragrances and can help him with picking the right scents in the future? Why didn't I just act like the many guys who come through the store every day and simply say, 'I think you're very attractive, can I have your number?'" Calvin had all these thoughts and more for days about this unsuccessful brush with fate. He hoped that the man would find a reason to return to the store and see him again, but no such luck.

Calvin began to use his employee discount to dress more trendy, careful to find clothes to accent the perfectly cut body he had refined by working out routinely at the free gym in their apartment building. He found that earthy colors like orange, burgundy, chocolate, and mustard were great compliments to his yellow tone and brown wavy hair. He was indeed "the shit". However, with all the confidence in his looks he was earning, he still longed to experience that true love Lavender wrote about. He began to believe that he would only experience love second hand, watching as Darnell and David lived the life he longed for.

Chapter 22

Although Calvin was very happy living with Darnell and David, he had begun to wonder if his presence put a strain on their relationship. So after a big dinner one Sunday in August 1991, he announced that he was going to be moving out and getting his own apartment. Both Darnell and David protested, telling Calvin that they loved having him there and that he was not financially ready to take on the responsibility of rent yet.

"Who's going to cook these meals now?" David said half joking, half serious. Both he and Darnell had become accustomed to grand dinners on Sunday and tasty quick meals throughout the week rendering foiled lunches that all their co-workers coveted on a daily basis.

"I will. I'm moving one floor down," Calvin said with a big smile.

"How are you going to afford that? This is a pretty expensive building," Darnell warned. He was always the voice of reason.

"This is a two bedroom apartment and I'm getting a one bedroom so it is much less expensive. I don't have a car to pay for. I don't have credit cards or any other bills. Plus, my commission checks are rocking. I make more in commission than I make on my regular check. I can do it. And I'll be right downstairs so I can see you two as much as you want to see me and I'll still cook for all three of us every day." Calvin was trying to sell his decision.

"I guess. But you don't have to cook for us if you're not living here. That's not fair," Darnell said.

"I love you guys. You are my family and I love cooking for you. If I don't cook for you, I probably won't be cooking at all. And it will be fair because I'll be cooking *your* groceries. You don't think I'm giving you this key back do you?" Calvin finished with a big laugh.

Calvin would indeed miss Darnell and David. They made him feel like a true part of their little family. Although the relationship between Darnell and David seemed more like playful brothers than lovers, the love between them was evident. It was the only example of a positive relationship Calvin had ever witnessed.

Chapter 23

"Come on Calvin, you have to do this. You are the best cook I know. And the way you make your dishes look, they could be put on a magazine cover. This is a big opportunity for you," Darnell pleaded.

Darnell was in charge of finding a caterer for his company's Christmas Party this year. He immediately thought of Calvin. A launch like this into the world of catering could change Calvin's life forever and Darnell knew it. He tried to convince Calvin as they lifted weights in the apartment building's gym. Unfortunately, Calvin did not have as much confidence.

"Darnell, you are tripping. You know I have never cooked for more than two or three people. And sure, you think my food is all that but how do you know that white people with money who are used to fine food will?" Calvin protested as sweat rolled down his back as a result of his strenuous routine.

"Man, I don't care if you're black, white, or purple, good food is good food. David and I will help you. This will be good money for you. You know you just moved and this money could pay your rent for a few months. Also, if this party is a hit, there will be people there begging you to do parties for them. This could be your break. Just think about it for a couple of days. Don't say no yet," Darnell insisted, now done with his own workout.

Calvin wrestled with the idea of catering for such a large event all night. He so desperately wanted to believe he could pull it off, but there was too much doubt. He now believed that his chance at a successful or prosperous life had been lost.

The next day at work he was lost in thought about the party when his thinking was disturbed.

"Excuse me Mister. Where can we find a suit for this gorgeous young man?"

A thick hipped, late middle-aged black woman in a mostly green, floral patterned, polyester dress stood before him. In tow with the woman was the cutest little boy Calvin had ever seen. The light skinned lad had hair not quite as wavy as his and bore only the slightest resemblance to the woman, obviously his grandmother.

"To get to the boys department, take the escalator up one floor in this section of the store," Calvin directed.

"Is someone getting a suit for Christmas?" Calvin further asked, hoping this was not the case. He imagined how much a young boy would hate to get a suit as a Christmas present in lieu of the now popular video games or a bike.

"No sir, we are getting a suit for the Fifth Grade Spelling Bee champion to wear to the State competition on Friday," the woman stated boastfully and grabbed the boy and kissed him on his yellow cheek. The young boy rolled his eyes half embarrassed, half proud.

"Well in that case, make sure Charles in the boys department doesn't try to sell you one of those overpriced gray or tan suits up there. Tell him Calvin said to show you that navy pinstriped Perry Ellis with the four buttons. That will be really nice with a gold tie. And it's on sale," Calvin advised.

With that, they both thanked Calvin and turned and headed for the escalator. The woman wrapped her fat arm around the boy's shoulders as they walked. As he watched them, Calvin wondered what his life would be like today had Gran been as genuinely proud of him as that woman was of her grandson. Where would he be

if Gran had fully supported him and encouraged him like that?
Would he be there selling clothes for a little more than minimum
wages if Gran had kissed him or hugged him from time to time?
But should he continue to accept this life as the end just because
Gran didn't do her part? Should he just curl up and die because
Paul was a cruel asshole?

Calvin shook himself back to life and immediately clocked out
for a break. On his break, he called Darnell who was now home
from work.

"D, I have an answer for you." Calvin started the conversation
without a greeting.

"What? An answer to what?" Darnell asked confused.

"I will do the party. I think, no I know I can cater that party.
I don't want to spend the rest of my life selling clothes and living
beneath my capabilities. I don't know why, but life is giving me
another chance and I'm taking it. I can't be sure this isn't the last
chance I'll have to live my dream."

Calvin worked untiringly for the week leading up to the party.
He made list after list of items for David to pick up at grocery, hobby,
and even fabric stores. Calvin did not intend to just prepare food;
he wanted the many tables he prepared to be themed, decorated,
and whimsical. With the budget he had been given, he figured
he could outdo himself with décor and food, and still profit more
money than he had ever seen at one time.

His hard work was well worth the pride he felt as he inspected
his tables just before the crowd began to arrive. He had employed
the services of David and a couple of his white co-workers from
Macy's to set up and serve at the party. Having a couple of white
faces on his team was a nice touch, adding legitimacy to his newly
formed catering business.

Although Atlanta's Christmases were usually anything but
white, Calvin had managed to create an environment he called,
"White Christmas" inside the rented ballroom. Each table was
loosely draped with silver satin material and covered with pearl-like

synthetic snowflakes. Throughout the room were white Christmas trees with all huge silver ornaments and white lights. All the food was in bite size portions and served out of gleaming silver serving dishes and chafing dishes. On one table was nothing but salads, already fixed in one serving bowls atop huge silver bowls filled with ice. Another much longer table was lined with heated chafing dishes of tasty morsels to satisfy even the pickiest eater. The desert table seemed to be the most remarkable of all loaded with colorful cakes, cupcakes, fingers snacks, and decorated cookies. The centerpiece of this table was a wonderfully elaborate gingerbread house decorated with white icing and jellybeans.

The effect of Calvin's decorated food stations was breathtaking. Everyone gasped in delight as they entered the room and each time, Calvin grinned ear to ear as he stood at the start of the food section in his black tuxedo and silver tie matching his décor.

By the end of the night, Calvin was glad Darnell had won their last argument. Darnell had business cards made for "Sharpe Events" and demanded Calvin have them on display at the party. Calvin protested, saying that advertising at someone else's event would be tacky. The compromise made was that Calvin would have the cards handy and would give each of his servers cards in case someone asked about the catering.

In the end, Calvin had given out over 100 cards and found out later that the three other servers and Darnell had given out at least another 100. The phone began to ring the very next day.

Chapter 24

Afterer that first Christmas Party for AHE Designs and it's high end clients, Sharpe Events was thrust into an almost overnight success, or so it seemed to Calvin as he looked back on the chain of events over the past few years. At one point, he thought he would never see any of his dreams fulfilled. Now at thirty-four, he sat at his art deco glass desk in his small rented office space in the up and coming Midtown Atlanta, deciding which companies or organizations he would have to turn away with requests for bids. He was one of the most sought after event planners in Atlanta, black or white. He now had an office staff of three, and an on-call serving staff of over fifty under his employment. It all seemed to happen with one courageous step instigated by a woman and a little boy asking for directions to buy a suit.

Calvin had defeated his fears, low self esteem, and bad circumstances to go against all odds and make a great life for himself. For his thirtieth birthday he had closed on a beautiful home in the historic black upper class district of Cascade. He owned two nice vehicles; one sport utility vehicle, practical for work, and one luxury car that just made him feel good. He had good friends, none as close as his dear Darnell and David who still were together and happy after all these years, but now residing prosperously in Washington D.C. Calvin had dated here and there as time and circumstance permitted, but never allowing himself the vulnerability of love again. The residue of his experiences with Zelda, Randolph, and Paul lingered and left him skeptical of anyone who came within his protected barrier. After one or two dates, he usually found reasons to not want to continue seeing a person. *"He's too skinny with his clothes off...He's too fat with his clothes off... He used to smoke so his lips are too dark... He's a republican... He's not a Christian... He's too Christian... He goes out too much... He never goes out..."*

"Calvin, we're going to have to move the holiday party for the Mayor next year. The George is telling us that they will no longer allow us to bring in our own food after this year." Tanisha, Calvin's assistant broke his concentration. Tanisha was chocolate, beautiful, slender, and was always dressed to the nines, whether she was meeting a client or not. Today she dawned a black mini skirt and matching long jacket and a red silk blouse.

"And they're telling us this today, one day before this year's event? They know we usually lock in next year's contract on the day before the current year's event. They are trying to get us to make a quick decision without weighing the options. Tell them we are not signing a contract unless we can bring our own food and servers. Period." Calvin felt good being able to make bold statements like this. He knew that dozens of hotels and banquet facilities longed to have events as big as the ones he catered come to their venues.

"Fine. They're also saying you'll have to meet with their manager on duty the night of the function to ensure we are meeting their safety standards." Tanisha half chuckled at this, anticipating Calvin's response.

"*Their* standards? We add class to that place just by having an event like this there. If it weren't for the great price and location, I wouldn't think of having it there in the first place. Are you kidding?" Calvin couldn't help but laugh too.

"I think they have some new General Manager who's not from here and doesn't know our reputation. Just shake the man's hand when you get there Saturday evening and tell him we'll make sure no fire exits are blocked." Tanisha consoled Calvin and left his office. She walked with a bounce that caused her six inch black pumps to clack against the hardwood floors and her perfectly placed ring curls to pop up and down against her shoulders.

On the Saturday of the Mayor's event, Calvin arrived early to oversee the set up of the ballroom and serving stations. He was fiercely orchestrating last minute details when he heard one of his crewmembers call his name. He turned to see the crewman pointing him out to a man in a nice black suit.

"Mr. Sharpe?" The man offered his hand and a beautiful smile. There was something familiar and charming about this man. His skin was the color of honey, smooth and even toned. He appeared to be in his early to mid twenties and was about an inch taller than Calvin. A man of his youth in a hotel of this caliber obviously was not the general manager.

"I am Zavier Jackson, Human Resources Director here at The George, and I'm the manager on duty this weekend. I was asked by our General Manager to meet with you this evening." The man was very articulate but not in an overtly annoying way. He was just obviously intelligent and well spoken.

"You know, this is probably inappropriate, but I think I know you from somewhere." Zavier seemed to bring this up out of nowhere. He squinted apparently trying to remember where he had met Calvin.

Normally Calvin would play along naming places and people until the natural laws of six degrees of separation kicked in; well knowing that this whole game was an over-used pick up technique. However, this time he actually believed he might have run across this man before; though he couldn't imagine not keeping in touch with such an attractive and intelligent man if he had.

"I know! Smell me," Zavier exclaimed, hardly containing his laughter.

"What?" Calvin couldn't believe this request.

"Smell me. Go ahead. What do you smell?" Zavier insisted.

Calvin obliged him. "Uh, smells like Escape by Calvin Klein. I know that because I used to…"

Then it hit him.

"Oh my God! How did you remember that? It's been almost ten years and it was just one encounter," Calvin said incredulously.

"It's been eight years to be exact. I remember because I was eighteen, just starting college. I have to tell you, I thought you were so attractive. And, by the way, you haven't changed a bit," Zavier said blushing slightly.

"Yes I have. I weigh at least twenty pounds more," Calvin offered.

"Maybe, but it looks like all muscle so I can't see it. As a matter of fact, you probably look even better, if that's possible." Zavier found himself more comfortable.

"You too man. You've toned up also I see. Why didn't you come back through the store after that one day?" Calvin asked.

"Man, I had just gotten to Atlanta to go to school and was flat broke. I couldn't afford to blow my MARTA pass going back and forth to Lenox Mall hoping to see a man who might or might not have been interested in me. When I did go back, you were never there so I gave up. I figured if it was meant to be, then fate would bring our paths together again. Who knew fate moved at a snail's pace?" Zavier explained.

"Look, I see you're very busy here. I have to stay here overnight as the manager on duty. Just call my room when you're done tonight. Room 832. It doesn't matter how late," Zavier said and turned to leave.

The rest of the night crept by and Calvin counted on his staff to mind the details of the party because his attention was totally distracted. He could only think about talking to Zavier again. Time simply would not go by. He felt as if his heart would beat right out of his chest if he didn't hear that articulate tenor voice of Zavier's soon. He felt like a teenager going on his first date.

Eventually, it became too much for him. Halfway through the event, he went to a house phone and dialed 7 then 832. The phone was answered on the first ring before Calvin could change his mind and hang up.

"This is Zavier."

"Hey. This is..." Calvin started.

"I know who it is." Zavier giggled like a kid.

"I just wanted to make sure you still want me to call when I'm done. Looks like it's going to be pretty late." Calvin could not come up with anything else. He had forgotten to think of a reason for the call before he dialed.

"That's not why you called. But yes, I want you to call. I really want you to come up to the room, but I'm not sure that's a good idea. I am officially at work," Zavier responded.

Calvin laughed. "You're right. Let's just talk tonight. Then maybe we can have lunch tomorrow."

"That sounds like a good plan. I can't wait."

Chapter 25

"Darnell, I really like this guy. I'm not sure what it is about him, but he's not like any other man I've met. When he suggested that expensive restaurant for our lunch date, I thought he was just like all the others who wanted to milk me for nice lunches, dinners, and presents. Then he blew my mind and paid for the whole thing." Calvin had immediately called Darnell to tell him about his first date with Zavier.

"Calvin, that one is a keeper. I don't think I've ever heard this much excitement in your voice about a man, especially after just one date. Now Calvin, I know you. Don't go looking for what's wrong with this man. Everyone has a flaw or two... or twenty. If you look hard enough, you will find something wrong. So don't go looking, this time just go with the flow and be reasonable. Do you think I like everything David does? Over the years, his one flaw has turned to one hundred, but I just adapt and keep moving because there is a man deep inside all those flaws that I'm still in love with," Darnell advised.

Although Darnell and David had long since moved to Washington D.C., Calvin was in constant communication with them, especially Darnell. He spoke to one of them by phone at least every other day. At least once every three months they would either visit Calvin in Atlanta or he would take a weekend trip to D.C. to spend time with them. Darnell and David had purchased a beautifully renovated brownstone *in Georgetown, one of the Capitol's most affluent communities. David landed a position as a principal architect with a large commercial firm in Alexandria, Virginia, a D.C. suburb, which dictated their move. David, refusing to allow Darnell's big break to be the separation of their relationship, gave up his recently promoted position with the Dekalb County Police Force to move with Darnell. After months of waiting for calls from the many law enforcement organizations in and around Washington D.C., David secured a small business license and placed an ad in a couple of local papers offering private security services. Who knew that private security was such a sought after service in D.C.? Within one month, David had more contracts than he could possibly service. He was forced to hire on additional officers, comprised mainly of recently retired police officers, federal agents, etc. Within a year, he leased out a whole floor of one of the buildings in the city to house his successful operation.*

"This time Darnell, I don't want to find any flaws. I think I like this guy just the way he is."

Zavier called Calvin later that night to tell him how much he enjoyed spending time with him at lunch. Calvin felt a soothing warmth throughout his body knowing that Zavier liked him as much as he like Zavier. Calvin remembered Darnell once telling him, "C, never let a man make you wonder how he feels about you." Zavier definitely intended to let Calvin know his feelings every step of the way. And this was wonderful.

Calvin and Zavier planned to meet for a very casual dinner the following Wednesday. Zavier told Calvin to dress down and wear comfortable shoes.

Zavier picked Calvin up in his Toyota SUV at his office. Calvin was more and more impressed by Zavier. He could not remember the last time someone offered to pick him up. Most guys either enjoyed the prestige of riding in Calvin's luxury cars, or felt their own vehicles were too subordinate to Calvin's to allow him to ride in. Zavier commented on how nice Calvin's new BMW was but did not show any immature reverence for it. Zavier seemed to be very comfortable with his own place in life and made the most of the life he had been given.

Zavier's charcoal suit, white shirt, and red striped tie were hanging in the back driver side window. He had changed into a blue and white Nike running suit with white Nike running shoes. Calvin had followed instructions and also wore his black fleece warm ups. When he hit the December night air before getting into the waiting SUV on Peachtree, he was happy he had chosen to wear fleece.

They went to a small, casual Italian restaurant on one of the small side streets in Midtown that Calvin, with all his connections and sophistication, had never been to. The tangy odor of red sauces and pasta's filled the little room. The food was great and the quiet, comfortable atmosphere matched.

"I have no idea what wine goes with what food, but honestly, I like sweet tea," Zavier confessed and laughed at himself.

"FYI, with pasta white sauce equals white wine; red sauce equals red wine. But you know what?" Calvin said.

"What?" Zavier asked, shining his beautiful brown eyes into Calvin's.

"I want sweet tea too," Calvin said as they both laughed.

Calvin loved being able to be himself with Zavier. He knew from their lunch on Sunday that Zavier knew very well how to handle himself in high-end social situations. But he loved that he could be plain everyday folk too.

After dinner, Zavier parked his SUV on a side street near Piedmont Park.

"Now we walk off that fattening dinner," Zavier demanded.

"What? We'll freeze," Calvin protested.

"It's not that cold. The more we walk, the warmer we'll feel," Zavier promised and grabbed Calvin's hand.

Calvin could not believe that this man was actually grabbing his hand on a public street. Moreover, he could not believe how good he felt letting him.

They walked the outer perimeter of the famous park. As the night sky overtook the day's light, men crept into the inner more tree-covered areas of the park. These men of the night looked around cautiously as they entered the darkness in search of temporary sexual satisfaction. Some were perverted older men looking for the young prostitutes who would suck their tiny dicks for a price. Others were the undercover "straight" guys who didn't dare go to a gay club or allow themselves the satisfaction of responding to a man on the street. Rather, they would gain their sexual pleasure under the protective anonymity the darkness provided.

Calvin and Zavier discussed everything from current events to celebrity gossip. Calvin was mesmerized as Zavier seemed to have an intelligent opinion on all topics. After walking the entire edge of the park, they found themselves back at the spot where they began. Calvin did not want the evening to end.

"The city is so beautiful from here. I have always been a fool for skylines," Calvin declared.

"Let's walk a few blocks on the street," Zavier insisted.

Zavier lead their charge to one of the taller office buildings. Since it was way after hours, there was a lone security officer at the lobby information counter.

Zavier hit the buzzer and told Calvin, "Give me your business card."

"Huh? Why?" Calvin asked, confused.

"Just give it to me, quick," Zavier insisted.

Calvin pulled a silver card from his wallet and handed it to Zavier.

"Can I help you?" The officer responded to Zavier hitting the buzzer.

"My name is Zavier Jackson, Director of Human Resources at The George down the street, and this is Calvin Sharpe with Sharpe Events. We are collaborating on having an event on your top floor in the large boardroom. We were just out for a run and had a debate over the ceiling height in that room. Do you think we could go up and look at it real quick?" Zavier explained with such sincerity that Calvin almost believed it. He held his and Calvin's business cards against the glass door as the guard walked over and inspected them.

"Uh, I don't know. I'm only supposed to let executives in after hours like this." The fat white man said looking suspicious.

"What are you doing? Let's just go," Calvin whispered.

"Come on. We are executives. If we looked different (if you know what I mean), I wonder would it be easier to get in there. It's not like we want to get into anybody's office. We just want to go straight up to the top floor and look around in that empty boardroom. There's nothing in there to steal. Do you know how much we are paying for that space? Mr. Warren would not be happy to know any of his employees did not cooperate fully with us," Zavier sounded sterner.

"O.k., o.k. There's no need to get agitated about it. Just sign in and leave your ID's with me," the guard conceded.

Zavier told Calvin to close his eyes as he opened the door to the boardroom. When Calvin opened his eyes, he could hardly believe what he was seeing. The entire far wall of the room was one big window showing the most breathtaking view of Atlanta's downtown skyline Calvin had ever seen. Zavier did not turn on the lights in the room so that the lit skyline would be even more magnificent.

"Oh my God. I never knew how beautiful Atlanta truly was," Calvin said and was forced to fight a strange urge to cry.

Zavier walked over closer to Calvin and as he stood transfixed on the view, he gently kissed the nape of Calvin's neck. Calvin inhaled abruptly in surprise and delight as Zavier's cool lips touched his neck. He turned around and looked at Zavier as if seeing him for the first time. Slowly, their lips met and they both knew they wanted to be together.

Their kiss seemed to last for only a minute or two, but time does fly when you're having fun.

"Oh man! Let's get out of here before that guard calls the police. It's been thirty minutes!" Zavier said.

Calvin invited Zavier to come home with him.

"Man, as much as I would love that, I really want to wait. I'll admit that I honestly can't remember dating a guy and not sleeping with him after one or two dates. But this time I really want it to be something different. I want you to know, Mr. Calvin Sharpe, that I'm falling for you and I'm falling way too fast for my taste. But I don't want to mess it up by having sex too soon. If I come home with you tonight, we *will* have sex and it *will* be good, but I want more. So it's worth the wait," Zavier said looking straight ahead at the street as he drove.

After Zavier took him back to his car in the garage near his office, Calvin thought about his evening all the way home. On his past dates, he had been to some of the most expensive restaurants in town, he had seen every good show at the Fox Theatre, he once had even flown to New York for a Broadway play. Now this man has come along and spent less than twenty-five dollars for dinner and spent the rest of the evening doing things that cost no money at all, giving him the best date he ever had.

Chapter 26

Calvin and Zavier began a ritual of calling each other at least every morning at the start of the day and every night before bed. Because it was Calvin's busy season, it was a challenge to see each other as often as they wanted, but they managed to share dinner or lunch every couple of days.

On Christmas Eve, Zavier went to Calvin's home for the first time. Because of Calvin's hectic schedule, they had usually met at restaurants or picked each other up from work to go on their time sensitive dates. However, Calvin had his last Christmas function earlier in the day and vowed not to work or even think about his upcoming New Year's Eve event until the day after Christmas.

When Zavier pulled into the circular drive, he was bedazzled. He almost expected a butler in tails and white gloves to open the oversized double door. He could hear the chime of the exaggerated doorbell go on for about a minute after he pressed the lit button.

"Since we're not having pasta, I didn't know which wine to bring," Zavier said, laughing and holding up two bottles of wine, one white and one red.

"It doesn't matter, I made sweet tea," Calvin responded with a chuckle.

"Looks like you made it just before it starts to rain. Come on in," Calvin continued.

The interior of the home was every bit as beautiful as the outside. Setting the stage for the grandeur of the home, there was a marble floored foyer just inside the front door with an antique royal bench, modest painting, and an oak table with a porcelain nativity scene staged on it, all dimly lit by the exquisite chandelier hanging above. Further inside, the skylight ceiling seemed to reach into the heavens exposing the overlooking second floor where Calvin's home office, TV room, and guest suite were found. The living room was done in warm shades of earth and was accented with afrocentric art and artifacts.

After they finished the light but tasty meal Calvin had prepared, Zavier and Calvin retired to the beautiful but comfortable living room for conversation. The light from the roaring fireplace and huge candles on elaborate holders were all that lit the room as some of R&B's greats crooned Christmas music in the background. This simple time together was the best Christmas Eve Calvin could remember.

The two laughed and talked the entire evening away. With them, the conversation was never at a lull. They both were so well versed on so many issues; it was like old friends talking whenever they were together.

"Mr. Calvin Sharpe, successful business owner, beautiful home owner, intellect; what else do you want out of life? What else is there for the man who has it all?" Zavier asked in a playful interviewing tone. Both men were sitting sideways facing each other on the overstuffed brown sofa in front of the crackling fire.

"I want to leave something in this world that lives beyond me; a book, art, an offspring, etc. I also want to really know what it is to love hard, and be loved more than I can imagine. I want to wake up every morning knowing that I'm not in this thing alone. I want to have one person who cares about every little detail of my life, just as I care about his," Calvin answered seriously, staring into Zavier's now moist brown eyes.

"You know, when I said I was falling for you... I meant, I am falling in love with you." Zavier almost whispered as he took a deep swallow, licked his lips, leaned forward, and delicately placed his lips on Calvin's.

After all the years, Calvin was reminded of the cool fall night when Randolph had first caused him to feel the sweet yet shocking sensation of a gentle kiss. Over the years, Calvin had become more mechanical in his approach to romance and sex. He normally would dispense with the foreplay or kissing as quickly as possible and go straight for the intercourse. Tonight, however, was different. He was enjoying this simple affectionate act more than he could remember enjoying oral or anal sex with anyone in many years.

A few moments into the kiss, Calvin slowly leaned back on the sofa and Zavier followed the lead and pressed his body against Calvin's as he reclined. As Zavier lay on top of Calvin, he could feel Calvin's erection growing in his corduroys. Feeling the thump of Calvin's huge dick jumping, begging to get out caused Zavier's own dick to grow and stiffen almost instantly. Zavier grinded his body against Calvin's so that their dicks danced vigorously with each other, building a sexual hunger that neither man would be able to control much longer.

Finally, Zavier lifted himself off the sofa and began to lift his tight fitting, red mock turtleneck over his head. Without uttering a word, Calvin grabbed his hand to stop him. The disappointment was easily read on Zavier's face. Then Calvin took Zavier's other hand in his and lead him across the hallway, passing the kitchen, to his huge master bedroom suite where a mahogany king sized bed with posts on every corner the size of Roman columns was positioned on a two step riser, with a purple velvet curtain swaggered behind it. Two mahogany nightstands rested on either side of the bed. It was the most regal bedroom Zavier had ever seen in life or on TV. The room was decorated in purple and silver. Calvin picked up a remote control device on the table near the door and clicked a button and a fireplace on the far wall in this room immediately came to life with a mild flame. He clicked another button and Chaka Khan's *Through The Fire* filled the room.

"Now, continue where you left off," Calvin said as he lifted his own white sweater over his head, exposing his ripped, yellow six pack. His nipples were still erect from the recent excitement. And as he continued to strip, it was evident that his dick remembered the earlier activities too, bobbing up and down in eager anticipation of attention.

"Damn, your dick is so big Calvin," Zavier said as he stared at the eleven inches like a hungry lion would look at a raw steak.

Zavier, now exposing his own honey colored toned body, dropped to his knees and began to suck Calvin on the spot. Calvin's head went back and his body stiffened at the sensation. First he worked at just the head and then moved further and further down until he had more than half of the giant appendage in his mouth. Calvin moaned in pleasure, affectionately rubbing Zavier's head as he stood leaning against the bedpost. Zavier now literally dripping with anticipation, rose to his feet and Calvin in turn sat in front of him on the bed. Calvin began to repay the favor. He licked Zavier's balls, kissed his inner thighs as Zavier's dick slapped him on the forehead. Then slowly he gulped as much of Zavier as he could take into his mouth. Zavier drew in a sudden breath, indicating to Calvin that he had hit on his spots. Calvin used this intelligence to his advantage and sucked Zavier as if his life depended on it. After several minutes, Zavier pulled himself out of Calvin's mouth.

"Man, you're going to make me cum," Zavier warned.

Calvin scooted himself up onto the bed and laid back. Zavier climbed atop him and kissed him. This time he was not gentle. He kissed him hard and madly like a hungry animal devouring his prey. Calvin rolled over under him and opened the small drawer on the mahogany nightstand and brought out a bottle of lubricant and a handful of condoms, some magnum sized and some regular.

Zavier's eyes followed Calvin's hand and his dick instinctively jumped in eager anticipation. Calvin returned to his spot beneath

Zavier, only this time he lay on his flat stomach. Zavier took the cue and began first to massage Calvin's perfectly round, tight butt. Then he poured some of the lube right onto Calvin's butt and began to finger it into him. He then chose one of the regular size condoms and put it on. Although it was a little tight, he knew that realistically the magnums were not his true size, and there was no sense in trying to be a show off.

Calvin laid with his eyes closed somewhat nervously waiting for Zavier to enter him. Although he was not a virgin by any means, his heart raced as if this were his first time. There was something about the way Zavier made him feel that seemed to restore the innocence to him that had been stolen so long ago. He was not "being fucked" or just having sex. This time, for the first time, he was making love.

Zavier entered Calvin slowly, only giving an inch at a time. Then slowly he began his smooth rhythm. Calvin groaned in pure pleasure as Zavier stroked him like he had never had it before. He was not brutal, nor was he slow and boring. Zavier leaned down and kissed the nape of Calvin's neck and never skipped a beat going in and out of Calvin. Without ever withdrawing, Zavier worked himself around so that he was pumping in and out of Calvin crossways, forming a letter 'T' with their bodies. Then he scooped Calvin's legs under him, and before Calvin could even realize how it happened, he was on his back with his firm muscled legs folded back to his head and Zavier still making sweet love to him. Although Calvin never before cared for this position, he loved being able to look into Zavier's eyes as he made love to him. And he loved thinking of it as making love, not being fucked. Anita Baker's *You Bring Me Joy* filled the room and spoke aloud what Calvin felt. This man indeed brought a joy that Calvin had never felt.

Just as Calvin thought he might cum while Zavier was in him, Zavier pulled out and reached over to the nightstand and got another condom and the bottle of lube. Calvin, already missing Zavier's dick but needing the break, laid his head back on the pillow and closed his eyes as he caught his breath. His dick was rock hard and standing straight up in the air with only the slightest curve upward on the end. He opened his eyes to see that Zavier had picked up one of the magnum condoms and was fitting it onto Calvin's dick. Calvin was silent and excited. Since leaving Paul, he had only been in the top position once or twice. He was not attracted to feminine guys, so whenever he met someone with which he wanted to have sex, they usually insisted on being the top.

After pouring lube on Calvin's stiff dick, Zavier lubricated himself and squatted over the yellow monster. He slowly lowered himself until the tip of the fat dick was stretching his hole and breaking through. Zavier groaned and grimaced but continued to lower himself. After he was about two inches onto it, he began to raise and lower himself and his face slowly changed from agony to ecstasy. Very gradually, Zavier found himself moving his butt's flesh closer and closer to Calvin's torso. Within minutes, Zavier was bouncing up and down and allowed himself to be filled with all eleven inches of Calvin's dick. Although it was painful, he was able to bear it and find joy in knowing that he had been a part of Calvin and now Calvin was a part of him. Zavier gloried in the knowledge that he and Calvin had bonded.

"I'm about to cum," Calvin declared between heavy breaths. Calvin could compare being inside Zavier to no other feeling he could remember.

Accordingly, Zavier slowly slid off Calvin's dick and removed the stretched condom. Calvin immediately began to masturbate as Zavier watched and masturbated himself kneeling between Calvin's legs. As if on cue, both Calvin and Zavier shot streams of hot white cum onto Calvin's stomach and chest. Zavier jerked spastically and Calvin struggled for breath as if in labor. Calvin peered past Zavier at the door, half expecting Gran to be there ready to destroy this magical moment.

Calvin and Zavier showered together in Calvin's walk in shower. As Calvin waited for Zavier to finish drying off he asked, "Do you still think you're falling in love with me?" He was ready for the worst.

"No," Zavier answered flatly. Once again, Calvin had experienced disaster immediately after giving himself to someone in sex.

"No?" Calvin clarified incredulously.

"No, I don't think I'm falling in love with you anymore. Now I *know* that I have completely fallen in love with you," Zavier declared matter-of-factly as he hung his towel, gave Calvin a quick kiss, and walked out of the bathroom.

Chapter 27

"Darnell, you guys haven't been here in over nine months. Ever since Zavier moved in you stopped coming to see me. Don't you like Zavier?"

"Calvin, don't be ridiculous. Of course we love Zavier. He is exactly what I always prayed you would find one day. But Zavier is part of the reason we haven't been there. With both of your busy schedules, when you get time off, the last thing you need is some old couple sitting around taking up your time to bond. We just thought we'd give you this first year to get used to each other before we visit again."

"Darnell, that's crazy. You know I love when you guys are around; and even Zavier has been asking when you're coming back. He really likes the idea of having a couple with so much in common with us as our best friends. He's so idealistic. He would love it if we all lived in one big house as a family. Trust me, you're not taking anything away from us by visiting as often as you can."

"Well I'll talk to David and see what his schedule looks like over the next few months. So how is the newly wed game going?" Darnell asked quickly changing the subject.

"D, Zavier is great. I had been living alone since I moved out of that apartment we all shared on Peachtree many years ago, so it would usually be hard to have someone around me all the time. Even when

I asked him to move in, I was afraid I would hate not having as much time alone as I was used to. But it's different with Zavier. I love coming home to him. Whenever I get home before him, I am miserable until he gets here. On weekends, Zavier insists that we do at least one thing apart and one thing together. Usually, I go shopping while Zavier does his Saturday afternoon bowling with his friends. Then we both rush home, get dressed and go out to a movie and dinner. That's if we're in town. Zavier loves to travel to the most unimaginable places. Last weekend, we just jumped in the car and drove to Chattanooga. Can you imagine? Chattanooga as a weekend getaway! But we had the best time. We went to the aquarium, had dinner on the Chattanooga Choo Choo, and saw Rock City. It was great. I never imagined there was so much to do in little cities like that. We've made weekend trips to Birmingham, Savannah, Charleston, Charlotte, and just about every drivable small city near Atlanta. He calls them mini-vacations and insists on having at least one a month." Calvin rambled on and on when he talked about Zavier. Darnell could see him smiling ear to ear through the phone. He was like a high school teenager in love for the first time.

"Well, I guess that answers the question of whether you're happy or not," Darnell said jokingly.

"Calvin, always remember these days. No matter how tough it may get, remember the joy of being with someone you love. You have no idea what traps a good man can fall into when he's not looking; but the important thing is to survive those traps. Just always remember to be honest, be forgiving, and be faithful," Darnell instructed solemnly before closing their phone call.

As Calvin placed the cordless phone on it's base, he sat in the black leather chair in his upstairs office and stared out at the small but well manicured back yard. *"…always remember these days."* He could hear Darnell's instructions resonating in his head. He would indeed always remember the peace he felt at this very moment. He thought back on all the terrible things he had been through realizing that he had no regrets. He realized that every happy moment along with every low place in his life helped to make him who he was today. And he was very proud of who he had become, so he could not regret the steps it took to get there no matter how painful they were. However, he began to wonder how many other young men in the predicament he had been in were out there today? How many teenage boys were wandering the streets because those who were supposed to support and protect them had turned their backs? He had been very blessed to run across Darnell in that dingy little hotel, but how many did not have anyone to look out for them?

He was snapped out of his deep thought by the pungent aroma of garlic that had made its way upstairs from the large, fully stocked kitchen below. Calvin now feared the entire house would stink for some time before airing out. He didn't dare hurt Zavier's feelings by saying anything though.

Zavier had insisted that since Calvin always cooked, he wanted to cook dinner this Sunday. Immediately after church, he pushed Calvin out of the kitchen, claiming he wanted no help. He was now downstairs trying his best to conjure up a meal that would come close to the delicacies Calvin prepared on a daily basis for them. His best attempt was to make the baked lasagna Calvin claimed to love although Zavier suspected that Calvin was only patronizing him. However, he labored over it just the same, praying that it would turn out as good as the first time he made it for Calvin shortly after they began dating.

The kitchen was an absolute disaster zone afterwards, but the dinner turned out very well. Zavier had fixed a nice garden salad and garlic bread to go along with his masterpiece lasagna. Although Calvin had taught him to choose a red wine with red-sauced pastas, he knew that they both would rather have sweet tea, so he had brewed a pitcher full. Sara Lee catered dessert in the form of a thawed strawberry cheesecake, which Zavier knew Calvin would love. Calvin always told Zavier that although he preferred homemade desserts, he loved Sara Lee's cheesecake.

"Zavier, this is a wonderful dinner. I'd better watch out, you might put Sharpe Events out of business with cooking like this," Calvin joked.

"Now why would I do that? I would be taking money out of my own pocket. Remember, what's yours is mine. And what's mine… is mine." Zavier laughed as a he took a sip of tea from his stemmed crystal goblet.

"Zav, after I hung up with Darnell, I thought a lot about my life. You know all I've been through and I'm very proud of who I've become. But I wouldn't be who I am or have the success I am enjoying if I hadn't had helping hands along the way. Lavender, Darnell, and David rescued me when I didn't know where to turn. Without their heroic acts, I just don't know if I would be alive today. Then you came along and rescued me in a different way and I realize it. I had no clue what real love looked like until you showed it to me." Calvin looked directly into Zavier's eyes as he spoke.

"Why so serious all of a sudden baby?" Zavier asked.

"I don't know. It's just been on my mind that I need to do something to help others now," Calvin answered.

"Baby, you help others all the time. You are one of the biggest givers in the missions programs at church. You volunteer at Hosea Feed The Hungry. Sharpe Events caters dinners for several group homes during the holidays for free. What else can you do?" Zavier questioned.

"All those things are very good for the many needy people they benefit. But I want to do something specifically for people who are stuck where I have been. When I left Woolfe, Mississippi in May 1982, it was raining; and for me, it rained until Darnell and David brought me home with them eight years later. I need to find a way to help young guys who have been abandoned by their families and don't know where to go or what to do to make it through until the sun shines again. I need to be the one to bring them in out of the rain," Calvin explained passionately.

"I understand Calvin, but why you? Why do you feel like you have to do this? I mean, what do you plan to do? Comb the streets for homeless boys and bring them home?" Zavier asked facetiously.

"If I have to. That is, if you support this. I need to do this, but I also need to know that it's o.k. with you. I have committed to you, and I couldn't do anything this important unless you support it. Zav, my life is truly good; but life is only full when you can give to others what has been given to you by God," Calvin said.

"Well, I guess I better go get the guest suite ready for stray boys," Zavier said half-heartedly. Calvin walked around the table and knelt by Zavier and kissed him as passionately as he ever had. He knew he had a man who would be with him through whatever life presented.

Calvin immediately went to work on his mission. With Zavier's guidance, Calvin established a nonprofit organization and called it OH!, an acronym for The Outstretched Hand Organization. Although a few of their friends volunteered to assist with the project, Calvin mainly drove the organization single-handedly. Zavier advised him that his target was too broad so he narrowed his vision and came up with a mission statement: *OH! is a not for profit organization dedicated to assisting young gay black men, ages thirteen through nineteen, who have been displaced, disenfranchised, disowned, and otherwise abandoned to find success through mentoring and locating proper resources for survival and positive development.*

Calvin loved OH! as if it were his own birth child. His new order of priorities were God, Zavier, OH!, and Sharpe Events. With that in mind, Calvin and Zavier decided to sell Taneisha twenty-five percent ownership in Sharpe Events and name her President as reward for her loyalty, dedication, and hard work. Calvin knew his passion for enterprise was dwindling as his calling for this new nonprofit venture was coming forth. Taneisha had new innovative ideas that would lead the company to new heights, and Calvin would still retain an overwhelmingly controlling interest, but with more of an advisory responsibility.

On the other hand, he was one hundred percent hands on with OH!. Calvin spent hours on end in his tiny, old office on the northwest side of Midtown near "The Beat". This was the area where young, misguided boys would prostitute themselves late at night to anyone from middle class men who felt too unattractive to get action any other way, to rich old perverts itching to get their wrinkled lips around a young black dick.

Calvin used his connections with some of the large corporations that Sharpe Events had relationships with to obtain very sizable donations and grants. He raised enough to actually hire a couple of employees and pay all the organization's operating expenses. Part of the organization's budget was set aside to provide housing for at least ten young men at a time during their time of transition. OH! linked with other agencies to train its clients valuable skills and get them jobs. Calvin, his staff, and volunteers placed flyers in free publications, bus stations, MARTA stations, on the street, in and around gay clubs, and anywhere potential clients may be. Within six months, OH! was up and running with a steady flow of young men in need of help. While Calvin was excited to be helping so many, he was saddened that there were so many who needed this kind of help.

Chapter 28

Many nights, Calvin would ride around areas where homeless or desperate boys were known to hang out and prostitute themselves. These young men would excitedly run up to his expensive luxury car when it slowed in hopes of turning a quick trick. Once he had their attention, he would offer them a way out of this demoralizing lifestyle through the assistance of OH!. Often he was cussed, threatened, and even spat on; but, every now and then, one of these misguided fellows would show up at OH! the next day, after having pondered the possibility of freedom all night.

On one such night, Calvin cruised the area around a popular eighteen and up gay club where many of the younger male prostitutes were known to work. On the corner was a thin, innocent looking, young man who looked no older than sixteen dressed in a pair of worn oversized jeans, a sleeveless t-shirt, a red baseball cap turned slightly left over his nappy hairstyle, and a red canvas backpack. Underneath the street costume he donned, a frightened and lonely kid seemed to be crying out to Calvin for help. As Calvin slowed Zavier's silver Mercedes SUV near the corner, the young man looked around nervously and approached the driver side window. Calvin drove alternate vehicles when he did this radical recruiting so that he would not be recognized by guys on the street who he had already pulled this disappointing stunt on.

"Wassup Daddy? What you looking for?" The kid tried to sound as 'thuggish' as he could, but it wasn't working for him. His voice was still way too high no matter how he tried to lower it.

Calvin's heart broke as he saw through this kid's mask of confidence.

"How old are you?" Calvin asked.

"What the fuck do you care? What do you want to do? I know you got the money," the kid answered.

"What's your name?" Calvin asked.

"Javon. Now can I get in or what 'cause I can't be standing here talking to you through no window if the cops come through here," Javon snapped with a little more attitude than Calvin liked. Calvin hit the unlock button and Javon took the cue and strutted around the front of the nice SUV and hopped in. Calvin pulled away from the corner driving aimlessly out of the vicinity.

"Now, let's talk business. What you looking for Daddy? I'll do whatever you want but I can't let you fuck me without a rubber. Anything else is cool. Oral is twenty dollars and fucking is fifty," The kid explained without emotion while looking around as if there may be a hidden camera or recorder inside the vehicle.

"Javon, I need to tell you that I'm not interested in having sex with you. I want to offer you a way out of this lifestyle. I know you don't want to be selling your body to…"

"Hell, the fuck no! You did not just pick me up right when it was getting busy to preach to me. Mutha-fucka, I could be making some fuckin' money!" The young man erupted.

"Javon, calm down. I just want you to know that there is an organization that's set up just to help guys like you get on their feet. For a couple of years now, we've been helping guys get it together when they felt like there was no hope. Just take my card and call me if… or when… you need me; because you will need me. This is 2003, and it's dangerous out here. This lifestyle cannot last son. I'm going to write my cell phone number on the back. There is something special about you and I don't want you to ruin your whole life on these streets. Call me whenever you need me," Calvin said with sincerity.

"Fuck you. You ride down here in the hood from your quiet suburbs in your big ass Mercedes trying to save the poor little street boys. Well, I don't need your help. I'm doing this because I like it. I'm doing this because I make damn good money doing it. I'm doing it because men will pay just to suck my dick. It's a win/win; I get my dick sucked and I get paid. So fuck you and your 'save the children' program. The children don't need you," Javon sneered.

With that, Javon opened the door and jumped out as Calvin was gliding to a stop at a red light. He slammed the door so hard that the entire vehicle shook. Calvin had run across a lot of resistance from some of the young guys he tried to help, but this one seemed to bother him more than usual. He called it a night, went home, snuggled as close as he could under Zavier's warm chest, and to his and Zavier's surprise, silently cried himself to sleep.

The next morning was a Saturday so he and Zavier sat down to a big breakfast. When he told Zavier about his encounter with Javon, Zavier pleaded with Calvin to stop his night campaign for OH!.

"Baby, you know I support you and OH! but I have to insist that you find a safer way to reach these guys. That maniac could have stabbed you last night. It's great for you to be there when these kids need and want it, but if they don't want to be helped, you can't force help on them. I don't know what I would do if you left here on one of those night crusades and didn't bring your yellow ass home to me. Baby, your love is what's flowing through my veins; it's what makes my heart beat. Without it, I could not breathe," Zavier said as he stared into Calvin's now moist eyes.

Chapter 29

"Wassup Daddy? What you looking for?" Javon gave his worn out introduction to a silver headed white man in a late-modeled black Lincoln Town Car.

The man looked to be in his late fifties or early sixties. He was thin and pale with blue veins visible even at night. Although it was spring, he wore a striped sweater over a white collared shirt and khakis.

The man's eyes lit up as if he had struck gold in the California mountains.

"I'm looking for a good time with a young buck who's not afraid to get a little wild. You game?" He smiled the smile of an old man offering a young boy candy to come home with him.

"Yeah, whatever. You know the deal right?" Javon said carefully, looking around for cops.

"What 'deal'?" The man inquired confused.

"Man, I'm not saying anything until you say it. I'm smarter than that. I'm not going to jail for nothing," Javon spat out.

"Oh! Yes, I know 'the deal'. I'll pay whatever you charge. I'm not a policeman. I just want to get my hands on that big black dick. It is big isn't it?" The old man started to fondle himself as he sat at the corner talking through his half open window to Javon.

"Yeah Daddy, it's big. I got nine inches for you to do whatever you want for … a hundred dollars." Javon hesitated and decided to up his price since the man had volunteered to pay whatever he asked.

"Whatever I want huh? Get in," The man instructed, licking his thin lips.

Javon looked around, surveyed the interior of the car, and swaggered to the passenger door holding his hugely oversized jeans up as he walked.

"Where we going?" Javon asked as he noticed the man heading for the I-75 onramp.

"Somewhere safe and private. Don't worry, I'm gonna take real good care of your little black ass." The man smiled wickedly as he answered. He reminded Javon of a villain in a horror movie.

"For real man, where you taking me? I don't want to go too far from downtown." Javon began to feel uncomfortable and slightly scared.

The man just got onto the highway headed north. Javon sat quiet for the duration of the ride until they finally got off the interstate about twenty minutes later somewhere in North Cobb County.

As they got off on the exit, the car ahead of them came to an abrupt stop at the turning red light. The sudden stop caused the Town Car to lunge forward and Javon noticed a black handgun slide from under the driver seat. The old man kicked the gun back under the seat with his foot and Javon pretended not to see it.

"Hey Daddy, what you want to do when we get where we're going?" Javon asked nervously.

"We're gonna play a little game and you're gonna earn every dollar you get for the next few days," The man answered devilishly.

"Few days?" Javon asked.

"Yeah, I'm not going back into the city until next week and where we're going, there's no other way back until I bring you.

Don't worry, it'll be fun," the man answered, seeming to enjoy the fright in Javon's voice.

Javon could hear his own heart beating in his chest. He was certain that this would be the end. This old white bastard was going to play sick sex games with him and then kill him. No one will ever know he's missing. This bastard will get away with it. His entire life played in his mind. He could see himself growing up in the small city of Tallahassee, Florida in the projects. He saw his mother working two jobs day and night just to feed him and his older brother. He saw his older brother watching before joining in as his friends took turns raping him two at a time, one in his mouth and one in his butt. He saw himself on the bus to Atlanta in search of a better way of life with the bundle of five-dollar bills he found under his brother's mattress. He remembered the desperation he felt when the money ran out so quickly and he had nowhere to go and could not go home.

Javon came to himself when the car rolled to a quiet stop at a red light. Without any thought or planning, Javon pulled the door handle to escape but the door was locked. The man noticed Javon's attempt and reached under the seat. The gun had slid out of his close reach giving Javon a few seconds to elbow the old man under his chin. The man's head snapped back and he groaned in pain. Javon struggled to locate the unlock button on the door and hit it just as the old man brought his hand from beneath the seat holding the gun. Javon opened the door and dove out onto the ground as the man fired a shot that came so close that Javon actually thought he was hit. He ran as fast as he could to the QT gas station on that corner.

When he reached the pavement just outside the store, he looked back noticing that the Lincoln had raced off into the darkness. There was shattered glass on the street from where the man had shot through the window at Javon. The young white attendant inside the store was stepping out of the freezer whistling as if nothing ever happened. If he told the attendant what just happened, he would be bound to call the police. What would Javon say to the police? What would he say when they asked why he was with this man in the first place? What would he say when they ask where he lives or what he does for a living? With that in mind, he decided to pull himself together and figure out how to get back to the city. He knew only one person to call.

Chapter 30

"Who is this again?" Calvin, still half asleep, asked the caller. He was attempting not to wake Zavier as he spoke.

"Javon. You remember, we talked a few months ago when you picked me up one night. You were trying to get me off the streets." Javon prayed Calvin would remember.

"Javon. Yes I remember man. What's up? Are you in trouble?" Calvin asked with genuine concern.

"Yeah, kinda. This old kat just tried to kill me," Javon explained as calmly as he could.

"What!" Calvin said, this time waking Zavier.

"It's a long story man, but I'm up here about twenty minutes up 75 and I need to get back. I ain't got no money and I don't know how long I can hang around this store," Javon explained.

"O.k. just stay calm. I'm coming to get you. Where exactly are you." Calvin decided to ask no more questions until he knew this kid was safe.

After figuring out where Javon was based on what he described around the area, Calvin started to get dressed.

"Baby, I'm going with you. This could be a trick. I thought we decided you would not ever give your personal number to any of these kids?" Zavier said sitting up in bed after hearing the gist of Calvin and Javon's telephone conversation.

"Zav, I know I shouldn't have given this kid my number, but I really felt like he needed me. And it looks like I was right. There was just something different about this one. I'm sorry for breaking the rules," Calvin repented.

"Well, I just want you to be careful baby. You're all I have and I love you. Wait for me to get dressed," Zavier replied.

"No Zav, I'll be alright. I'm very sure this is no trick. I could hear the fear in this kid's voice. He has to be in real need to have called me so I don't want to scare him off by showing up with someone else. I promise I'll call you when I get him in the car to let you know I'm o.k.," Calvin said.

As Calvin pulled into the lot at the QT, he searched for Javon but did not see him anywhere. It was almost four o'clock in the morning and there was no one in sight. As he pulled into the parking space, Javon darted from the side of the store and ran up to the passenger door. Calvin could see the obvious relief in Javon's eyes as he hopped into Zavier's Mercedes SUV. Calvin had intentionally drove the same car he was driving when he met Javon to make it easier for him to recognize him.

"Are you o.k.?" Calvin asked before putting the vehicle in reverse.

"Yeah, I'm cool. 'Preciate you coming to get me." Javon tried to sound calm.

"I told you I would be here for you and I meant it," Calvin replied and headed for the onramp.

Calvin decided not to pressure Javon for details yet. He figured the kid needed to gain comfort with him before opening up, so neither he nor Javon spoke for several minutes as they drove.

As they reached the city Calvin spoke. "Where do you want me to take you?"

"You can drop me off at the bus station," Javon answered in a surprisingly humble tone.

"The bus station? Where are you going?" Calvin asked.

"I'm not going anywhere. That's where my stuff is. I have a locker in the station," Javon answered.

"So where do you sleep?" Calvin became more concerned.

"Here and there. I get in where I can fit in. You know what I'm saying?" The old, want-to-be cool Javon returned.

"Yes, I know what you're saying. You're homeless," Calvin said with sadness in his voice.

"I ain't no bum, dude. I'm just between places right now. I'm cool." Javon started to become slightly defensive.

"Javon, I know you're not a bum. You may not believe this, but I've been there man. When I was probably about your age, or a little younger, I had just gotten to the city from a small town and had nowhere to go. I didn't know what to do and probably would have been doing exactly what you do for money if this special person hadn't been there to give me a hand. That's why I'm so determined to give you a hand. I want you to overcome this situation and one day reach down and help someone else up. Do you want to sleep in a real bed tonight?" Calvin asked sincerely.

"Yes," Javon answered simply, speaking no other words. He kept his eyes focused straight ahead on the highway as Calvin drove through Downtown Atlanta toward the historically elite Cascade Community in Southwest Atlanta.

"You're what?" Zavier asked incredulously.

"I'm bringing the kid home with me, baby. He doesn't really have anywhere else to go." Calvin's stomach churned in nervousness, praying Zavier would go along with this risky plan.

"Calvin, is he in the car with you right now?" Zavier asked.

"Yes," Calvin answered trying to keep Javon from knowing that there was some debate about him going home with Calvin.

"Then I guess you can't really talk about it. And I guess you've already made this decision, so I don't know why you're even calling me now." Zavier was obviously not happy about this new turn of events.

"Can we talk more about this when I get there?" Calvin asked.

"There's nothing to talk about, you've made the decision without my input or support; that's something you said you would never do. So, goodnight Calvin, I'll be asleep when you get here. Try not to wake me," Zavier said and disconnected the call.

That conversation worried Calvin immensely. He and Zavier had never really had an argument. If they disagreed, they would calmly talk it out and work out a compromise. He knew he was wrong here but there was no time to discuss this with Zavier first. What was he supposed to do? Should he have said, "I want to keep you from sleeping in the bus terminal tonight after you've already had a traumatic experience, but let me call my lover and discuss it with him for half an hour and maybe I can help you." No, he had to make a decision right then. Zavier needed to understand that. Calvin was caught between his commitment to OH! and his commitment to Zavier.

When Calvin and Javon got home, Calvin fixed Javon a snack of leftovers and juice in the kitchen, and nervously went up the stairs to the bedroom. As promised, Zavier was wrapped under the brown duvet with his back turned and face in the pillow. Calvin had lovingly spent enough nights watching Zavier sleep to know that he was not truly asleep now.

"Zavier," Calvin said gently, still standing near the door.

"Zavier. I know you're not asleep. Listen, I know you're angry but I want to talk to you. We agreed that we would never let a situation get bad enough that we couldn't talk about it. We also agreed we would never go to bed angry," Calvin reminded.

"We also agreed that no one would ever spend the night in this house unless we both agree. We also agreed that you would not do anything that endangers yourself for the sake of OH!. So please don't try to remind me of the rules or 'agreements' because you've already starting breaking them." Zavier spoke but never turned his face to Calvin.

Calvin walked over and sat on the bed.

"Baby, I'm sorry. That's all I can say, I'm sorry. If you want me to go take that kid to a hotel and check him into a room, I'll do that. But I can't leave him out on the street homeless. I have been there and I know the fear he is feeling. I wish I could explain it, but I just can't do it. I love you, and I'll do whatever I have to in order to make sure you are happy, but please don't ask me to abandon my mission to help this kid," Calvin pleaded.

Zavier sat up and looked Calvin in the eyes.

"Calvin, I understand your need to help. Trust me, I am here to support you in that. If you said you wanted to build a house made of cornbread, I would go out and buy all the meal, eggs, and flour I could find. But I just want you to be safe. These are street kids you're dealing with. They have been conditioned to do whatever it takes to get over. Your intentions are great, and OH! is a wonderful organization that I'm proud to be a part of, but you just have to do things wisely. Now, it's too late with this kid, I'll just have to trust that he won't rob and murder us. But this is the last time one comes home, ok?" Zavier said as he grabbed Calvin's face and pulled it in close to his by his ears.

"O.k. I love you so much Zavier Sharpe," Calvin said and gave him a short kiss.

"And I love you, Calvin Jackson," Zavier returned.

They often switched last names mocking a struggle for head of the household. The truth was they actually had created something that few couples can ever achieve, a fair and equal relationship.

Chapter 31

"Zavier, you need to just tell Calvin to get that kid out of your house. It was nice to bring him home the first night. It was generous to let him stay a week. But now, a month later, it's gone too far. His little ass needs to go," Darnell said in no uncertain terms.

"I know Darnell, but Calvin is very passionate about helping this kid and I don't want him to think I'm not supportive. You know Calvin has a bleeding heart for anyone in need. It's bad enough that we argued about it when he first brought him home. I don't want to go through that again and have Calvin feeling like he's in a relationship with a heartless person," Zavier said.

"That's bullshit. You better get that boy out of your house before he either steals, destroys your relationship, or becomes so comfortable that you can't get him out easily," Darnell said.

"Well, I don't think the first two things will happen, but I'm afraid it's already too late for the third. Javon is totally at home. He says he's trying to find a job, but I honestly don't think he leaves the house. There is a bus stop at the end of the block, but he says he doesn't have transportation to get to most of the interviews OH! sets up for him," Zavier explained.

"Now this is a kid who used to sell his ass for enough change to get on MARTA and now he feels too good to ride the bus to a job *interview? Zavier, you and Calvin have to know when you've done all you can for someone. Don't worry, I'll talk to Calvin about this,"* Darnell decided.

"No! Darnell, I'm begging you, please don't. I don't want Calvin to think I have something bothering me and can't talk to him about it. It will hurt his feelings. And I'm not talking to him because I don't want to discourage him. I'll fix this, just give me some time," Zavier pleaded.

"O.k., but don't take too much time. It just might cost you," Darnell warned before hanging up.

"Javon, tell me what happened to you the night that I brought you here. I didn't want to pressure you about it, but it's been a while now and I really want to know," Calvin asked as he and Javon sat on the sofa watching music videos.

Zavier had gone upstairs when Javon flipped the television to music videos. The rap music Javon loved was of no interest to Zavier or Calvin. However, Calvin feigned interest in an effort to relate to Javon. In his idealistic mind, Calvin felt that it was only a matter of time before he cracked the code and actually reached Javon. He had visions of Javon making his motivational speech to a room full of kids, explaining how he was at the bottom of the rope before he was saved and his life turned around. He imagined Javon carrying his leather briefcase into his top floor office where a photo of Calvin sat on his desk to inspire him to reach for the stars.

"Man, that shit was fucked up," Javon started.

"Javon, I asked you to try to use better language here, remember?" Calvin inserted.

"My bad. Anyway, it was 'messed' up," Javon corrected himself.

Javon told the story in gory detail. And to Calvin's amazement, Javon began to cry as he told it. Calvin too went to pieces seeing the pain on Javon's face. Javon went on to tell how he had been molested over and over by his brother and his brother's 'boys'. He told him how they did more and more disgusting things to him each time they raped him. What began as one boy forcing Javon to suck his dick escalated over the next couple of years to several boys taking turns entering him and then all of them standing over him masturbating on him as he lay in the middle of the dirty floor.

This story painfully reminded Calvin of the sexual torture he himself had endured at the hands of Paul so many years ago. Calvin grabbed Javon in his arms and hugged him tight, rubbing his back and kissing his forehead. Javon became a small child in Calvin's embrace allowing him to rock back him back and forth almost to sleep. After what seemed to be a long time of holding Javon, Calvin relaxed his grip around him. Javon then drew back a little and began to kiss Calvin's neck. Calvin stiffened and inhaled a sudden breath and his head jerked back at the pleasing shock. He allowed Javon to continue for a moment then came to himself.

"Whoa! Javon, what are you doing?" Calvin asked, trying not to raise his voice.

"I'm doing what you want me to do," Javon answered and attempted to continue his work on Calvin's now red neck. As a matter of fact, his entire face was now red.

"I do not want you to kiss me. That's not why you're here. As a matter of fact, I'm not sure you should be here much longer, son," Calvin said solemnly.

"Stop calling me son. I ain't your fuckin' child," Javon snapped and went into the guest suite.

Calvin felt guilty although he had done nothing wrong. Although he was worn and weak from the emotional strain, he sat up late hoping to avoid having to talk to Zavier. Zavier always seemed to know when Calvin was keeping something from him, so if he just didn't see him, maybe he would never know.

Eventually he went up to bed and as planned, Zavier was fast asleep. He quietly climbed in bed and pecked a kiss on Zavier's cheek before drifting off to sleep himself. That night, Calvin dreamed he was making love to Zavier. He dreamed he was first kissing, then sucking, then penetrating Zavier gently and passionately. In the dream, they switched places and it was time for Zavier to top Calvin as he lay on his stomach. At first, Zavier was as gentle as Calvin had been, kissing his neck and whispering how much he loved him in his ear with each glide in and out. Then he became less gentle, moving fast, and rough. Zavier began to slap him hard on his butt, and pounced on him like an animal. As he thrust in and out brutally, he said harsh things like, "take this dick bitch", "I'm tearing that yellow ass up", "I'm gonna cum all up in that tight ass"… Then Zavier began to cum and Calvin could feel it explode inside him. He and Zavier had always used condoms and pulled out when they climaxed, so this shocked him. He turned his head around and there was Javon, breathing hard as he pulled his long, limp dick out of him.

Calvin flinched as he woke from this pseudo-erotic nightmare.

"You o.k.?" Zavier asked with his eyes still closed as he threw his arm around Calvin.

"Uh, yeah I'm fine. Go back to sleep," Calvin answered.

Calvin tossed and turned the rest of the night, not really getting any sleep. Consequently, the next morning, Calvin decided to sleep in and just go into the Sharpe Events Office in the afternoon for a meeting. As the sun rose, light poured into the bedroom from the French doors leading to the bedroom deck overlooking the back yard. He was too tired to get up and pull the blinds so he just buried himself under the many pillows on the bed and the overstuffed duvet. He awakened to the sound of his bedroom door opening and footsteps walking across the room. He froze still to hear what was going on. He knew Zavier had a staff meeting today so there was no way he would come back home in the middle of the morning. Javon must have assumed that Calvin had left at his usual time. The bed had so many pillows and the duvet was so thick that Javon would never notice the lump under the covers which represented Calvin's muscular body. Calvin heard drawers opening and closing and decided enough was enough.

"What are you doing?" Calvin startled Javon now holding two watches in his hand.

Javon looked as guilty as the cat that swallowed the canary. He was only wearing a towel and was dripping wet. He apparently thought no one was home and decided to violate Calvin's and Zavier's privacy while he dried off from his shower. He immediately dropped the watches back into the antique jewelry box on the dresser.

"I was just looking around," Javon lied nervously. His voice was high pitched and he spoke the words too fast.

"Looking around? In my bedroom?" Calvin questioned suspiciously.

Calvin noticed Javon was carrying Zavier's ragged green duffle bag he kept in the garage, and it was full.

"What you got in that bag?" Calvin asked, eyeing it.

"Just my stuff. You said I have to leave so I borrowed this bag to put my stuff in." Javon began to visibly perspire.

"Can I see what you have Javon?" Calvin spoke calmly, trying not to let his suspicion sound through.

"Man look, you can have it all back. I just wanted to take some stuff so I could survive on the street. Here, you can have it." Javon gave in.

Javon tossed the bag on the bed and Calvin picked it up. He had packed it with a blanket, a couple of tee shirts, potato chips in a can, the coffee can filled with coin change that usually sat atop the refrigerator, and a framed snapshot Zavier had taken of Calvin raking leaves.

"Javon, you could have asked for all these things and we would have gladly given them to you. You don't have to steal. And, you don't have to be on the streets. I can get you some housing through OH!. You just have to follow the program guidelines and get a job. We are not here to pay your way through life. We're here to help you pay your own way…legitimately," Calvin told him compassionately.

Calvin was sitting up in his bed with the covers now thrown back wearing only his boxer briefs. He hesitantly extended his open arms signaling Javon to come to him for a hug. Javon silently obeyed the beckon and allowed his slender frame to fall into Calvin's strong arms. He lay his head on Calvin's shoulder and stretched his body out over Calvin's on the bed.

Calvin knew this was dangerous and he tried his hardest not to allow his dick to stiffen, but he was powerless against this force of lust. Javon felt Calvin's erection and began to glide his body over it. Javon surreptitiously removed his towel and took up where he left off last night kissing Calvin's neck. Calvin parted his lips and let out a short breath of pleasure at the touch of Javon's tongue on his neck. Javon skillfully licked his way from Calvin's neck to his nipples, from his nipples to his waist, and from his waist to his dick. Once he freed Calvin's massive dick from his underwear, he sucked as if his life depended on it. Calvin laid back pumping his hips up and down and Javon took huge gulps of his dick. *Where did this boy learn to take all eleven inches into his throat like that?* He wondered. Calvin did not allow his mind to think about how wrong this act was, he simply wanted to enjoy it.

Javon took a break, lifted his head, and asked, "You think I can have a hundred dollars?"

Calvin couldn't believe his ears. He had rescued this kid from almost being killed, brought him to his home, upset his partner, fed and sheltered him for over a month, overlooked his stealing from him, and now he was trying to get a hundred dollars by having sex with him?

"You ungrateful whore. Yeah, I'll give you a hundred dollars, but if you want to work for it, then you can. Then I want you to leave this house and don't come back. Now turn on your stomach," Calvin commanded with an anger and vulgarity that he didn't even recognize in his own voice.

Calvin reached in the drawer of the bedside table, grabbed a magnum condom, fitted it on his giant hard dick, and poured lube on Javon's tight round butt, allowing it to ooze down the crack into his hole. Without any gentleness or concern for Javon's pain, Calvin forced his big dick into him. Javon gritted his teeth in an attempt not to cry out as Calvin rammed him. Calvin began to relive his dream, but this time he was on top brutally and savagely sexing Javon. Calvin used all the language from the dream.

"You want to be a whore? Well this is what whores get. Take this dick all up in your ass, you bitch!" Calvin seemed to be possessed by someone or something else.

Calvin flipped Javon over onto his back in one quick motion. Without missing a beat, he re-entered Javon's hole, lifting his legs far in the air, and continued pounding him as if this sexual act was his punishment for wrongdoing. Just as Javon thought he could no longer take it, Calvin snatched his dick out of him, removed the condom and crawled up over Javon squatting over his chest. Before Javon could shield himself, Calvin's cum shot all over his face. Hot bullets of semen dripped from Javon's cheek, nose, and even over his lips.

Calvin immediately seemed to be released from his evil trance. He collapsed beside Javon and covered his face. He could not believe the events of the past few minutes. He walked over to dresser, opened the top drawer and took a crisp one hundred dollar bill from his wallet.

"Here. Take this and get the hell out of my house," Calvin said as he threw the money on the bed, still not breathing at his normal pace.

Javon folded the money in the palm of his hand, wiped his face with the towel he previously wore, grabbed the duffle bag of stolen goods, and ran downstairs. Within five minutes Calvin heard the alarm chime from the front door opening and closing. He rushed to the control panel to change the alarm code and collapsed on the floor sobbing like a small child.

Chapter 32

"I can't believe this happened. It was like I had no control of myself. Darnell, now I have to wonder do I really want to help these kids or do I just want to be close enough to them to fantasize about them. I'm so confused," Calvin confessed to Darnell.

"Calvin, don't be silly. That punk seduced you and you were weak. That's all to it. Sure, you should have kicked him out a long time ago, but that doesn't make it alright for him to use his body to get what he wants from you," Darnell answered.

"Yeah, but I feel like such a failure. I feel like I have let down every young man who has been through OH!'s doors. Channel Seven News wants to do a human interest piece on OH! and on me, but I can't do that, I'm a hypocrite. I run a program that is supposed to protect young men from being sexually abused; a program designed to teach these guys that they don't have to sell their bodies for money to survive. Then I turn around and brutally misuse a kid's body and pay him for it," Calvin explained in a defeated tone.

"Calvin, I know this is big but you have to let it be a mistake of the past and move on. Mr. Perfect, it is o.k. for you to make mistakes. Johon, or whatever that whore's name is, will be fine. Trust me. This guy is a survivor. He is trained to do whatever it takes to survive. Unfortunately, sometimes it takes hurting himself and others. Calvin baby, helping a person goes only so far and then it crosses the line.

And just across that line is a place called codependency. You have got to know when to say when," Darnell instructed in his most fatherly tone.

Darnell continued without allowing Calvin to speak.

"Now, the most important thing is protecting your relationship. What are you going to say to Zavier?" Darnell asked.

"Well, I don't know. I thought about just not saying anything and letting the whole thing blow over," Calvin said.

"I think that's a mistake Cal. You and Zavier have a real bond and when two people have a connection like that, they each know when something is not right with the other. I'm afraid Zavier will know you did something and find himself suspicious and not trusting of you. A relationship can survive a lot of things, but distrust is not one of them. Just tell him you made a horrible mistake and ask him to forgive you. I really believe that you and Zavier have enough love for each other to move on past this," Darnell advised.

"Thanks D, I don't know what I would do if you were not there for me. Please hurry and make those arrangements to come here before I get on a plane and show up there. It's been way too long," Calvin said before ending the call.

As Calvin sat in his home office chair, he looked at the framed photo of him and Zavier displayed on his desk. He reflected on Darnell's advice, fighting an inner battle over whether to tell Zavier of his indiscretion with Javon or not. If he chose not to tell him, how would he explain Javon's sudden departure? It is one thing to not tell Zavier something, but it is another thing altogether to tell him something that is untrue. In the end, he decided to take heed to Darnell's instruction and tell Zavier the whole sick truth.

He looked at the clock and realized that he had been on the phone with Darnell for over two hours and it was nearing time for Zavier to be home. He appreciated the fact that Darnell had taken so much time to listen to him. Calvin knew that Darnell's days were very fast-paced and he would be very fortunate to get more than five minutes of his time on a telephone call.

Calvin raced to the bedroom to change the sheets and wash the ones currently on the bed. Although he planned to tell Zavier what happened, he did not want him to actually see the spots where cum dripped onto the sheets and pillowcase from Javon's young face. He threw together an easy meal of baked chicken, mashed potatoes, green beans and cornbread, and was setting the table when Zavier got home from work a few minutes early.

"Hey baby, what are you doing here?" Zavier asked cheerfully.

"I should be asking you the same thing? You're home early," Calvin responded.

"Yeah. Not much going on at the hotel so the staff meeting was short, which allowed me to get the rest of my work done early today. How was your day?" Zavier asked happily.

"I'll tell you all about it over dinner. Go put on something comfortable and we'll talk. The food is ready." Calvin rushed Zavier off.

Calvin had set the mahogany dining room table but thought better of it and decided the smaller round glass table in the bay window nook off the kitchen may provide a more intimate and calming environment for this massive load he was about to dump on Zavier. There was still plenty of sunlight shining brightly through the huge sloping window, so he forewent lighting candles at the table. He set the table with powder blue dishes, faint yellow napkins, light green frosted goblets, and lavender placemats. He had read somewhere that pastel colors were peaceful and relaxing. He needed every peaceful force he could conjure up for this conversation.

As they ate in silence, Calvin battled internally, urging himself to start the conversation and just get it over with. Every time he got up enough strength to speak, fear held him back. He did not want to see the hurt in Zavier's eyes when he told him that he had cheated. He picked at his food with no real appetite.

"This is a good meal, thank you," Zavier said somewhat flatly.

"Thanks. It's nothing fancy. I didn't have a lot of time," Calvin responded giggling somewhat nervously.

"I don't know why not, you've been home all day," Zavier snapped back shocking Calvin.

"How did you... why do you say that?" Calvin asked totally surprised.

"Because I called Sharpe Events for you and Taniesha said you didn't show up for their meeting. So I called OH! and no one there heard from you either. You didn't even call either of them," Zavier explained.

Zavier's voice did not carry the concern Calvin would have thought it should have. Zavier hesitated a moment and looked Calvin in the eyes with a solemn look on his face.

"Calvin, did you have sex with Javon today?" Zavier asked in a shaky voice and took a deep swallow.

"Why are you asking me that?" Calvin skirted around the question, but his eyes filled with tears as he stared into his plate. He could no longer look at Zavier.

"Because this is the first meal we've had in over a month without Javon scarfing down as much as he can. Because I went in the guest suite and there is no sign of Javon or any of his things. Because this is the first time you've gone a whole hour without mentioning his name to me. Because when I left home this morning there were solid blue sheets on the bed and now the sheets are blue but they have little diamonds embossed on them. Because I cleaned up two days ago and arranged your condoms on one side of the drawer and mine on the other so it would be easier to find the right ones in the dark, and now they're all scattered together again. Finally, because you're sitting there red as Rudolph's nose crying like somebody died," Zavier surmised.

With that, Zavier scooted his high-back fabric covered chair out, threw his napkin into his plate, stood, and walked away.

"Baby, wait. Let me explain," Calvin urged, standing to follow Zavier.

Zavier stopped in his steps.

"Explain? What you gonna explain? How you brought a little whore into our home against my wishes? You gonna explain how you fucked the kid that you wanted me to think you were 'helping'? A kid who is sixteen years younger than I am and *twenty-three years younger* than you...a teenager! Oh, I know, you'll explain how you fucked him in the same bed you fuck me in. Is that it? Maybe I'm wrong. Maybe he fucked you. Well either way, spare me the explanation. I'd rather not know," Zavier said with brutal sarcasm as he continued walking toward the bedroom.

"So what now?" Calvin asked, his sight now blurry with tears.

"I'm going to get a few things and head back to the hotel," Zavier responded still walking with his back turned.

"You just left there. What are you going to do at work tonight?" Calvin asked.

By this time Zavier was standing at the door to his separate walk in closet in the master bedroom. He stopped to face Calvin as he answered his question.

"I'm going to check in until I can find somewhere to live," Zavier responded gravely.

Chapter 33

"I don't know what I'm going to do. I can't believe that a few minutes of insanity has cost me the best thing that ever happened to me. Darnell, I thought I would spend the rest of my life with Zavier. People said that male/male relationships cannot last forever and we were determined to prove that wrong. After all, look at you and David. How could I let one stupid absence of mind ruin my life? I honestly don't know where to go from here. I haven't been to Sharpe Events since Zavier left and I can't imagine that I could ever face those kids at OH! again after what I've done to Javon," Calvin lamented.

"Calvin, pull yourself together boy. You know you're stronger than this. They say that sometimes bad things happen to good people. Well, sometimes terrible things happen to wonderful people. Javon was a terrible thing and he happened to you and Zavier. I'm still not sure your relationship is over. This is not the worst that could have happened. Have you tried talking to Zavier?" Darnell asked.

"I've called him on his cell phone all day every day. I don't want to repeatedly call his office but when I do call, he politely says goodbye and hangs up as soon as he recognizes my voice. I thought about showing up at the hotel but I know how he hates drama at work. So I know that would only make him regret me even more. You know Darnell, I really believed it when you said our relationship was stronger than this," Calvin said in his most defeated tone.

155

"Cal Baby, trust me. This too shall pass and no matter how it works out with you and Zavier, you are a strong man who has come through much more than this. You can and will rise to the top. Watch and see," Darnell encouraged.

"Yeah, I have been through a lot but I have never loved anyone this much so this hurts far worse. I don't know if I'll rise to the top with this one Darnell. Can I come spend some time with you guys? You and Zavier are the closet people in my life. Now that Zavier is gone, I won't be able to make it through this without you," Calvin explained.

"Sure, just let me talk to David and get a plan together and we'll take care of you. Don't make your flight arrangements yet. I want to make sure we're going to be in town first," Darnell answered before ending the call.

"Good Morning, this is Zavier Jackson."

"Hello Zavier."

"Darnell, I know why you're calling and I really don't have time for this. I..."

"Zavier, Calvin has too much class to show up at your office and act a fool. I don't. I will jump my ass on a plane and be there before you leave today and stand in the middle of that nice hotel lobby and let the whole world in on all your business," Darnell threatened.

"O.k. Queen, you have my attention for a few minutes," Zavier said, laughing slightly as he gave in to a very persistent Darnell.

"I should have David beat your ass for calling me a queen but I'm going to let that one go since you're hurting and all," Darnell said, laughing with Zavier.

It gave Darnell great joy to hear Zavier laugh. Despite Zavier's stubbornness and act of nonchalance, Darnell knew the pain he must be feeling.

"Zavier, you're right. I do want to speak to you about Calvin. I know you say you don't want to talk about it, but I know you do. I know you need to have someone you can share all this madness with so you can get past it," Darnell began.

"I just can't believe he did that to me... to us. I have never loved anyone as much as I love Calvin. I took the greatest risk I have ever taken and committed myself, my life, to him. I trusted that man with my heart and he took it and broke it. How am I supposed to get past that?" Zavier said seriously.

"Zavier, I wish I knew the answer to that. All I know is that you have to move past it and you have to forgive Calvin and pick back up where you guys left off. You guys..." Darnell started.

"Are you kidding?" Zavier cut Darnell off before he could go further.

As much as he wanted everything to go back to the way it was, he could not forgive Calvin's transgression.

"Calvin brought a teenage hooker into our house, fed him, cleaned him up, and fucked him in the same bed we slept in. He thought that changing the sheets and cooking a nice dinner would make everything all better. Are you kidding?" Zavier tried to keep himself composed and his voice low, knowing his office was poorly insulated and his staff would surely hear every word if he yelled like he wanted to.

"Zavier, I hear you. I do. There is no way I'm going to attempt to excuse or defend what Calvin did. But I do know that he did not plan it and he was not himself when he did it. And most important, he is sorrier than he has ever been in his whole life. Calvin has been through a whole lot in his life, and I'm sure that has a lot to do with the terrible mistake he made. But again, I'm not going to try to rationalize it. Zavier, it was a mistake; a terrible mistake mind you, but still a mistake. Can't you even try to forgive Calvin? I don't think you will have to worry about anything like this ever happening again. He is lower than I have ever seen him, and I've seen him pretty low. I don't think he would ever risk going through this kind of pain again," Darnell pleaded with Zavier.

"Darnell, I hear everything you're saying but I don't think you can understand what I'm feeling. You and David have that storybook relationship so it's impossible for you to really get it. I know you mean well," Zavier said softly.

"Zavier, you're forcing me to pull out the big guns," Darnell began.

Darnell took in a deep breath and audibly exhaled for half a minute.

"When David and I first moved to D.C. in the ninety's, David tried and tried, but could not find a job so I was pretty much supporting the household while David was at home. I knew that being unemployed had lowered David's self esteem and had him somewhat depressed so one day I decided to take off work early and take David to dinner and a movie, you know, just to get him out of the house. I called out for David when I entered the house because I knew how he hated being startled. He did not answer so I figured he was out on an interview; he had one every other day. I went upstairs to the bedroom to change clothes and what I found there changed our lives. There was some young bastard laying on his back with his legs in the air while David fucked him. And that wasn't the worst part. David never allowed me to even play with his ass because he was all top and could not imagine being penetrated. Yeah, right. Well as he was fucking the kid on my bed, an extremely muscular guy was fucking David. You got it, David cheated on me with not one, but two men. I recognized the muscular guy as the man I left installing cable TV weeks prior to this. After I got the gun from the closet downstairs, made the two guys hit the streets butt ass naked in the middle of the day, and broke everything breakable in the house, I allowed David to try to explain. Apparently, the cable man had come back a few days after the installation and propositioned David. David turned him down the first few times, but the man was persistent and came by whenever he was in the neighborhood. Finally, one day he showed up with a younger, softer looking guy in tow, assuming David would offer less resistance if there was someone he could top.

He apparently was right. According to David, there were three encounters like this." Darnell paused to hear Zavier's reaction.

"I cannot believe my ears. I can't believe Calvin never told me this," Zavier said, dragging out each word carefully.

"That's because Calvin does not know and I don't want him to know. I never wanted anyone to know because I guess in some ways I feel embarrassed. I would not have told you this if I wasn't pulling out all the stops to get you to see that I do understand," Darnell said.

"Why would you be embarrassed? David's the one who cheated," Zavier asked.

"Because most people would say I'm a fool for letting him live, not to mention letting him live with me. And under normal circumstances I would definitely agree. But I loved this man too much to not do everything possible to not have to give that love up," Darnell admitted.

"But how could you continue to be with someone who abused your trust?" Zavier asked.

"It was not easy but I knew I had two choices. I could throw him out and live alone and in pain for who knows how long, or I could try to understand that David didn't cheat because he didn't love me. Hell, he couldn't have been doing it because he was in love with someone else; there were *two* other people. David had always been in control of his life and prided himself on hard work. Being unemployed messed with his mind and caused him to suddenly feel powerless. Having sex with those guys gave him a small sense of power for the few minutes it lasted. It was like drugs to him. Sex with me could not give him that. As a matter of fact, being with me reminded him that I was supporting him and often made him feel that sex was one way of paying his rent. At least that's what the counselor said," Darnell said.

"Wow Darnell, I had no idea. But I'm glad it all worked out for you guys and you were able to move on and not have to deal with any aftermath of that foolishness in your future. I just don't know if I can," Zavier said.

"But we do have to deal with the aftermath of that foolishness. We did get past that with counseling, understanding, rebuilding trust, and a lot of love. But it is literally costing me my life. Zavier, David was diagnosed as an HIV carrier about a year after that incident. He encouraged me to get tested and I was diagnosed positive. Now David is just fine, but I don't think I will live much longer. Calvin keeps pressuring me to come there and today he said he wants to come up here. I can't let him see me this way. I don't look the same; I've lost over fifty pounds since you've seen me. I can't walk without assistance and it takes all my strength to carry on telephone conversations without sounding feeble." Darnell began to sniffle and his voice cracked.

Zavier lost it and broke down crying but continued to hold the phone to his ear.

"Zavier, even with all that I'm going through, I don't regret forgiving David. There is no greater feeling than loving and being loved by the person you know you were meant to be with. Because David is by my side, I am not afraid to face this death. I only worry about those I will leave behind me. My mother died years ago and I am not close to my sisters. All I really have is David, Calvin, and now you. Please don't make me have to worry about Calvin being alone. You and I are all he has and I'll be leaving soon. Give a dying man his last wish and forgive Calvin and try to work this out," Darnell pleaded.

"I'll think about it," Zavier conceded.

"I knew that 'dying man's last wish' thing would get you," Darnell said, trying to laugh through his tears.

Chapter 34

As Calvin sat in the large overstuffed leather chair by the downstairs bay window looking out on the well-landscaped backyard, he mentally began to diagnose himself. *I must be clinically depressed, or maybe this is a nervous breakdown. Maybe I should call someone. I'll call Taniesha tomorrow and ask her to get me an appointment with the doctor. I'm too tired today, I'll call her tomorrow,* he thought as he felt the stubble of straight hair on his face from not having shaved in three days. He could smell his own tart odor and realized he could not remember whether he showered yesterday or not. He definitely had not showered today. His usually low cut hair had begun to grow out into a curly afro since he missed his usual barber appointments for the past two weeks.

Calvin had instructed one of the receptionists at OH! to schedule volunteers to cover his duties. He also told Taniesha that he would be taking a couple of weeks off to rest. When he attempted to check the voicemail on his home telephone, to his dismay the mechanical female voice announced, "YOU HAVE... THIRTY-NINE... NEW MESSAGES." At that point he hung up the phone, too weary to hear all the messages of concern and worry from his staff and friends. By now, there would be over fifty messages. He only answered his personal cell phone, knowing that only Darnell, David and Taniesha had the number since he had changed it to keep Javon from attempting to call him. Taniesha was included on this elite list solely because Calvin had asked her to facilitate the number change; he did not have the strength to deal with a long customer service call these days. Calvin planned each night to wake up the following morning, get dressed, and reconvene his normal, productive life. However, each morning, he decided to do it "tomorrow".

"You look a mess." The voice startled Calvin as he instantly turned to see if he had completely lost his mind and was now imagining voices.

"Zavier. Where did you come from?" Calvin asked, not knowing what to say.

It was like heart resuscitation from a defibrillator when Calvin saw Zavier's strong, handsome face. He was immediately shocked back to life by this man's presence.

"The doorbell has been disconnected. Did you do that?" Zavier asked showing more concern than he intended.

"Yes. I didn't want to be bothered," Calvin answered softly.

"Calvin, no one can reach you by telephone and you won't let anyone in the house. That's not a good idea. What if there's an emergency?" Zavier asked.

"If someone is sick, I'm not a doctor so no need to call me. If someone is dead, it's too late anyway. So what is an 'emergency' anyway?" Calvin theorized.

"Don't be crazy, Calvin. You know you can't just seclude yourself locked up in this house like this. You stink, your breath stinks, your hair is a mess, you're wearing clothes that look like you slept in them all night, and you don't look like you've been eating. What is wrong with you?" Zavier asked in a frustrated but concerned tone.

"What's wrong with me? You're kidding right?" Calvin asked half laughing.

Zavier had come over to talk to Calvin and try to decide if he really wanted to resume a life with Calvin. He wanted to feel sure that Calvin truly regretted what happened. After seeing him in this state, he had his answer.

"Calvin, I want you to go upstairs, shower, and shave. I'm taking you somewhere to get something to eat. I'm going to call the travel agency and book the first cruise we can get on. It doesn't matter where it's going as long as we can leave Atlanta tomorrow. Is your passport here or at your Sharpe Events office?" Zavier asked as if there had been no time between them.

"Uh, it's here. But..." Calvin began.

"Calvin, there are no 'buts'. We're doing this. We need to do this, ok?" Zavier said as he grabbed Calvin's hand lifting him to his feet.

Calvin's whole body tingled at the firm grip of Zavier's strong hand. He had not had physical contact with another human in many days and the sensation was startling and strangely erotic. He felt his dick harden as Zavier pulled him into his chest and hugged him tightly.

"Now please go shower and brush your teeth. You stink so bad that I refuse to kiss you now," Zavier said laughing and patted Calvin on his behind.

Calvin smiled ear to ear as he relinquished Zavier's grasp and bounded off toward the master suite.

"Oh Calvin," Zavier called.

"Yeah?" Calvin stopped mid-stride.

"As soon as we get back from the cruise, we're going straight to D.C. to see Darnell," Zavier announced in such a tone that Calvin knew the issue was not open for debate.

The weight of despair had miraculously lifted from Calvin and he went from depression to delight in a matter of minutes. As he continued his path to the shower, he marveled at the ever-surprising power of love.

At the door leading into the bedroom, he turned and saw that Zavier was watching him as he walked. He paused, staring back.

A single tear rolled down his face as Calvin repeated Zavier's quote from a few weeks earlier: "Your love is what flows in my veins and causes my heart to beat. Without it, I could not breathe."

Chapter 35

"Now can we turn our phones on?" Calvin asked as the light rail train approached the baggage claim area at Hartsfield-Jackson International Airport, which boasts the distinction of the world's largest airport, and was recently renamed to honor Maynard Jackson's contribution to its success.

The cruise had been the exact healing experience both Calvin and Zavier needed. Calvin was back to himself, and while it would take time for Zavier's wound to fully heal, he knew he definitely was willing to work through it because he recognized that he wanted to spend the rest of his life with Calvin.

"I don't understand you Calvin. I found you just a week ago refusing to answer any calls or check messages. Now, you can't wait to get in the car to see who called. Go ahead, turn your phone on. I just didn't want us to think about business while we were on vacation," Zavier said as the two rode the long escalator up the mountain-sized incline from the underground rail to the Terminal North baggage claim.

Zavier was unaware that Calvin had secretly checked all his past messages one night when they were docked in the Bahamas, so he only had eight new messages on his business phone and none on his personal phone. Two were from Taniesha, just checking in; her voice a lot calmer than her previous messages since Zavier had called her to inform her of Calvin's well being. One was from Darnell who must have just awakened when he called because his voice was only a broken whisper. There were three calls from David, who probably wanted to set up the details of their surprise trip to D.C. to visit Darnell tomorrow. Finally, there were two calls from a guy with Channel Seven News, trying to set up an interview with Calvin. The man said that Calvin's voicemail at OH! was full and one of the volunteers at the office had given him this number to try to reach him. Calvin made a mental note to put out a memo to all volunteer receptionists at OH! to never give out his cell phone number to anyone other than staff and clients.

Calvin and Zavier waited at carousel D for their luggage for half an hour before the last few bags were claimed. Calvin's bag was one of the first to come down the belt, but Zavier's was a no show. After standing in line for twenty minutes and speaking with a customer service representative, Zavier was assured that his bag would be on the next flight from Miami which was due to arrive in forty-five minutes, the last flight of the night.

"Let's just stay here and wait for it. It's already after eleven and neither of us will feel like coming back here in the morning before our flight to D.C. It's no big deal, we can have late supper in one of the restaurants here and I will remotely check the voicemail at OH! because one of the callers from my cell phone messages said it is full," Calvin suggested.

Zavier gave in to the plan, too tired from travel and unbelievable love making to fight. Calvin attempted in vain to access his voicemail remotely. The mechanical voice alerted, "THE PASSWORD YOU ENTERED IS INCORRECT!" upon each attempt.

"Damn! I really need to clear those messages before going to D.C. and I know I'm not going to have the time tomorrow. Now I wish that I had made all my passwords the same so that I could easily remember them," Calvin thought out loud.

He decided to leave a message on the voicemail of the Channel Seven reporter so that he would have it first thing in the morning and not feel that Calvin was not interested in the interview. As Calvin waited for the voicemail to pick up, he blew kisses at Zavier who responded by tickling him and threatening to mess up his attempt at leaving a professional message.

"Human Interest, this is Siri." An articulate, tenor voice answered.

"Oh, hello. I'm sorry, I was expecting to leave a voicemail message," Calvin explained his clumsy greeting.

"We work very late in this department some nights. How can I help you?" The man replied.

"My name is Calvin Sharpe, and..." Calvin began.

"Yes sir, Mr. Sharpe. You are a hard man to get a hold of. My name is Siri Dawson and I'm the one who was trying to reach you. You may have been notified before that we are interested in doing a segment on your organization?" The man said.

"Yes I did know that and I'm sorry for the delayed response, I had some personal matters to attend to. Unfortunately, I will be out of town again for a few days starting tomorrow. When did you want to interview me?" Calvin asked.

"Oh, I'm not a reporter. I just need to verify some information, ask you some general questions, and set up the real interview with you and the team," the man responded.

"Well with that voice and phenomenal diction, you should be a reporter," Calvin said.

"Thank you very much Mr. Sharpe. I am only doing this job because I want to be a reporter some day," the man responded with pride in his voice.

Calvin answered the man's generic questions about the proper spelling of his name, his title with OH!, and names of kids they could contact for supporting interviews.

"Mr. Sharpe, when we received the lead to report on OH!, I did some personal research into the organization and you. I want you to know that I am so honored to have spoken to you tonight. As I face challenges while growing in my career and in life, I will think

167

of great men like you as role models. Thank you for what you are doing Sir," the man said in a serious and sincere tone.

"Wow! Thank you, Mr.? I'm sorry, I don't remember your last name," Calvin said, now feeling the moistness rolling from the corners of his eyes. He was slightly embarrassed that such a simple compliment could bring tears to his eyes. At this point in his life, he really needed to know that what he was doing mattered.

"Dawson, Siri Dawson. And there's no need to thank me. In the media, we thrive on the bad things our people are doing. I just wanted to let you know that I personally admire and honor the good things you do," the man said.

"Well, I don't know what to say but if you ever need anything or just an ear to listen, you can indeed call me," Calvin said.

"Be careful, I'll make you my mentor and drive you nuts for advice," The man joked before ending the call.

When Calvin ended the call, he felt an even greater sense of renewal. He felt forgiven for his transgression with Javon and now was able to take OH! to all new levels of service. Once Zavier's luggage arrived and they had retrieved their car from the airport lot, Calvin insisted it was imperative that he drop Zavier off at home and go to the OH! office to clear those messages.

"What if some kid is in trouble and trying to reach someone for help?" Calvin pleaded his case.

"Calvin, then they will hit '0' and get a volunteer," Zavier quickly responded.

"I know, but some of these kids will only talk to the person they met first, which is usually me," Calvin countered.

"O.k., I told you I am in full support of OH! but you are not going to that office alone tonight. We can go there now before we go home. Deal?" Zavier asked in compromise.

"Deal," Calvin answered, satisfied.

Chapter 36

"You don't have to baby-sit me. You just sit here and watch the car. This isn't the best neighborhood to leave a new BMW on the street you know. I'll run up there, listen to the messages really quick and be right back. I promise I won't try to act on any of the calls, I'll just write them down to attend to later. O.k.?" Calvin told Zavier as they sat on the side street adjacent to the building where OH! had it's offices.

"Fine, but I'm coming to get you if you're not back in fifteen minutes," Zavier threatened playfully.

"Yessir Boss!" Calvin played back.

"I love you Calvin," Zavier said as Calvin opened the passenger door of the white BMW seven series sedan.

"I love you more," Calvin responded.

Zavier felt his heart warm when he heard those words from Calvin. *"There goes the man I love with all my heart,"* he thought to himself as Calvin walked briskly around the corner of the building jangling a large ring of keys.

While Calvin checked his messages, Zavier decided to turn his cell phone on and check the messages he had missed while away on the cruise.

Calvin's new mentee was correct. His voicemail box was indeed full. He quickly journaled all the calls on a legal pad, trying his best not to be alarmed by any of the messages so that he would not feel the urge to respond to them tonight. As a message from one of his colleagues with the Heart to Heart Foundation regarding a possible joint venture played, he glanced out the window overlooking the street on the opposite side of the building from where Zavier waited in the car. He noticed a very familiar red backpack on a young man at the corner. It was Javon, back on the streets. Calvin hit the speaker button to release the playback of the messages and went down the stairs and out onto the street. He decided that he should formally apologize to Javon and let him know that OH!'s services were still available to him, but he would need to work with one of his staff or volunteers.

As Calvin exited the building door, a black Lincoln Town Car cruised by him slowing at the corner where Javon stood. Javon slowly approached the tinted driver-side window of the Lincoln, looking around before making his move. Calvin noticed a strange look on Javon's face when the window lowered a quarter of the way down. Javon stepped back slowly, walking backward and never taking his eyes off the car. Javon shook his head from side to side as he spoke to the driver.

"What the fuck do you want with me? Leave me alone!" Javon was now yelling.

Javon stopped in his backward steps and began to slowly move closer to the car again. This time, his face and voice did not indicate anger; instead, Calvin recognized the look of stone cold fear on Javon's face. Until this point, neither Javon nor the driver of the Lincoln had noticed Calvin standing near the entrance of the old brick building that took up the short block.

"Hey!" Calvin shouted in the general direction of the car.

At that moment, Javon glanced in Calvin's direction and broke out in a rapid sprint around the corner. The car door opened only a few inches and under the streetlights, Calvin saw the shimmer of metal. He looked around to see if there was anyone else on the street who could be hurt, and in that split second, he heard the quick pop of a lone firecracker. The car sped off down the now quiet street and Calvin felt relieved that he had scared off Javon's possible attacker, but was frightened that the shot fired may have hit Javon in his run for safety. Because his head was turned, he did not see where the bullet landed.

Zavier found that he only had a few messages. His hotel staff had left a couple of trivial questions and then there were two from David asking Zavier to call the minute he got the message. The last message caught his attention.

"Zavier, this is David. I know you guys won't be back until tomorrow and it is not fair to tell you this way, but Darnell is gone. He died yesterday very peacefully. He knew he was leaving and he wanted me to tell you and Calvin that he loves you more than he could ever say in words. He said to tell you that you and Calvin, along with me, are his real family and he hopes that you will not burden yourself too much over his passing. I know this message is too long, but I can't stop talking because when I hang up this phone I'm going to have to sit in this house alone and I just can't stand to do that right now, so I'm sorry for taking up so much of your voicemail time. You know people keep saying he's in a better place. I know that! He's fine, but what about me? He's in a better place, but I'm in the worst place a person could be; alone in this fucking big house where everything here has his touch, his scent. I..." David's voice choked and the message stopped.

Zavier sat in stunned silence and the tears would not stop rolling down his face. As he closed his eyes and laid his head back against the cushioned leather headrest, he heard the quick pop of either a car backfiring or a gunshot. He quickly wiped his face with the back of his hand, looked around and got out of the car. He decided to disregard Calvin's request and go upstairs to make sure he was alright. He was happy Calvin had given him a key to the front door of the building and a key to the OH! office. However, he had not decided whether to tell Calvin about Darnell now or later at home. He dreaded that fact that the news would be devastating to Calvin.

At least Zavier knew about Darnell's condition and impending demise. This would be a total shock to Calvin about the closest person in his life other than Zavier.

Calvin braced himself for what he might see and began to walk toward the end of the corner. As he walked, he realized that he must have been gripped by fear more than he realized because he could actually feel his legs going out from under him. He took three steps and fell to his knees. He felt a sudden sensation to throw up and when he opened his mouth and retched, a smooth liquid erupted violently as he coughed and struggled not to choke on it. Although the street was fairly well lit, everything seemed to grow dark. He heard Zavier cry out his name in the distance behind him. *"Oh good, Zavier will clean me up and get me off this street before someone sees me like this,"* he thought. As the sensation to cough or throw up stopped, he rubbed his now burning chest and although his hands had little feeling, he knew something was wrong. He pulled his hand away and drew it up to his eyes struggling to see in the ever-darkening light. He saw the blood and now knew what the burning was.

"Calviiin! Noooo! Baby noooo! Don't leave me! Please don't leave me! Who did this? I love you." Calvin faintly heard Zavier's voice growing further and further away.

Just before the darkness completely overtook his sight, a moment of visibility was allowed. Zavier's strong, handsome face was all that Calvin could see and "I love you" were the last words that he heard.

Epilogue

"I know what today is and wanted to make sure you were o.k.," Zavier said.

"Man, I don't know how to feel. Sometimes I miss him so much. Can you believe it's been two years already?" David asked.

"Trust me brother, I know. Remember, today is your day but in two days it will be mine. Man, a couple of years ago I would have never imagined that you and I would be having this conversation. What happened? We had the best lives and best relationships imaginable. Now all that is gone. All taken away in a couple of days," Zavier lamented.

"Yeah, that was the toughest time I have ever had in my life, and I've had some tough times. I can still remember every detail of both funerals. It was a trip having Darnell's funeral one day and then having to go through the whole thing again the next day for Calvin; although Calvin's funeral was a whole different kind of event," David said.

"I know. I tried to keep it low key, but the media played it up so big that there was no way to minimize it. It's funny, once Calvin was killed, he was finally recognized as the hero that he was every day. I mean everyone showed up for that service. Even the mayor was there, and I can still hear her great words about Calvin and the work he did with OH!" Zavier was lost in his own recounts.

173

"Yeah, it was something. But we did a good job with Darnell's service too. Thanks to your help, we gave him just what he had requested, a quiet, dignified memorial service in Atlanta," David said.

There was a silence on the line as both David and Zavier each momentarily relived the day that he had sat in the awkward seat of the grieving partner. Each man had to fight his inner self to rightfully claim the seat. There was an unspoken concern that the funeral attendees questioned the legitimacy of a grieving male partner. At Darnell's funeral, David, who had always kept his sexuality and relationship private, struggled with the knowledge that Darnell's family resented him and his legal power of attorney where Darnell was concerned. So at the funeral, they were forced to follow in the processional line of family behind this man whom they had no respect for; this man who, in their minds, had killed Darnell; this man who now placed legal claim on all the valuables and money they should be scouring Darnell's home for.

The struggle Zavier faced at Calvin's service was different. He had to fight the temptation to scream as one speaker after another honored Calvin as a single man and referred to Zavier as Calvin's good friend.

"So how is OH! going these days?" David inquired, reconvening the conversation.

"Man, Calvin's death brought so much attention to OH! that it is one of the largest non profit organizations in the city. The scope of its mission has been widened to include straight boys and girls since there is much more funding and staff available now. I still make it my business to go by the office once a week to check on things. Mainly, I go there because seeing Javon working so hard and giving such dedication to the organization sort of keeps Calvin alive for me. You know he is taking night classes to earn a degree?" Zavier beamed.

"No! Who would have thought that little trick would even finish high school? I'm just glad the little speech he made about changing his life because of Calvin was sincere. I'm also glad you didn't kill him

174

on the spot for just running up to the podium to speak without being on program at the funeral," David joked.

"Right! But now I'm glad he did. It was the most moving moment of the day for me," Zavier admitted.

"Alright, well what's up with the love life?" David asked.

"Love life? Man do you hear me going on and on about a man who's been dead for two years? I don't think I have room for anyone else in my heart right now. I've tried to date, but it always feels strange," Zavier said.

"Man, you know I understand, but you owe it to yourself and to Calvin to try to move on and make yourself happy again. It can happen," David advised.

"Wait. Are you dating someone?" Zavier asked accusingly.

"Actually Zav, I may be in love again. I want you to come to D.C. and meet her. She is a political advisor to one of my company's highest paying clients," David said proudly.

"Her?" Zavier responded shocked.

"I knew you would respond like that, but you knew I never stopped being attracted to women. You are my family now man and I'm counting on you not to trip," David said.

"Does she know about Darnell?" Zavier asked cautiously.

"I don't think that's any of her business. I told her that my past is complicated and we both agreed that what's in the past should stay in the past," David rationalized.

"David, I have no problem with you having a relationship with a woman, but I just don't think it's a good idea to keep something as big as your own sexuality a secret from someone you say you're in love with. How are you going to explain your HIV status to her?" Zavier considered the appropriateness of the question but concluded that it was too important and must be asked.

"Man, you know I'm asympthematic. I'm never sick and my body is 'tite'. Hell, I look better than most of these guys in their twenties these days. So there's no need to even bring that shit up yet," David said nonchalantly.

"Are you fucking kidding?" Zavier became somewhat irate.

"David you know I love you, but you are being an unrealistic dumbass. I am very disappointed in your attitude about this. You know what we've been through with Darnell. Do you really want to put someone else at risk without them even knowing it?" Zavier cautioned.

Again, there was dead silence on the line. When David spoke, his voice was soft and each word was pronounced slowly and deliberately.

"Zavier, I just don't want to be alone anymore. I have tried to find a man to be with, but every time I meet someone I am attracted to, either he turns out to just want to have sex or I begin to feel guilty as if I'm cheating on Darnell. Only when I date women do I actually get to know them before they get my dick and run off to get the next one. Dating women doesn't make me feel like I'm trying to replace Darnell. I don't know, maybe I'm not in love but at least I'm not lonely anymore. Can't you support me on this?" David asked.

"D, you are my brother, I do love you, and I definitely understand your loneliness; but I can't support you on this one as long as you are not being honest with this woman. I feel like I would be dishonoring Darnell's memory by doing so. I can't go along with you trying to hide the fact that he ever lived; the fact that he helped to make you who you are today. If nothing else, his death financially changed your life," Zavier said, immediately regretting it.

"Are you accusing me of staying with Darnell only in hopes of getting the life insurance money? I'm not the only one that cashed in pretty big that week you know," David replied.

"No, I'm accusing you of forgetting that money was not why you stayed," Zavier said before hanging up. His heart was heavy as he wondered if he had lost his last true confidant.

Zavier had called David from his office at the hotel. He was stuck as Manager on Duty for the weekend again, which reminded him of how his and Calvin's relationship began. As he made his way to the lobby making mental notes to have the engineer turn the air conditioning up a little, he dreaded his responsibility to meet with the contacts hosting the big black tie event in one of the hotel's beautiful ballrooms.

"Excuse me, Mr. Jackson?" The articulate, clear voice came from behind him. The voice reminded Zavier of pure spring water flowing over fine crystal.

"Yes, I'm Zavier Jackson," Zavier replied as he turned to face this attractive young man.

"Mr. Jackson, they told me at the front desk to see you regarding media access to the event tonight. My name is Siri Dawson with..." The man started.

"Yes I know, with Channel Seven News. I've seen you on TV," Zavier said, shaking the man's hand and smiling broadly.

"Thank you for recognizing me. I've only been on television a few weeks so it still fascinates me to be recognized," the reporter said, laughing and pumping Zavier's hand.

"Well, let's get you set up in here," Zavier said, walking the gorgeous light complexioned man and the now trailing camera crew into the ballroom.

"They get the prettiest boys they can find to put on TV these days. They must know that in Atlanta, if you put a light skinned, muscular pretty boy on, your ratings will double," Zavier thought to himself as he watched the man patting his curly deep brown fro.

As Zavier sat at his desk the following Monday afternoon, he appreciated the fact that working over the weekend as Manager on Duty had given him the opportunity to catch up on the mounds of paperwork that usually donned his inbox. This allowed him the time he had been hoping for to review some resumes for a couple of open positions. He was disturbed by the ringing of his desk telephone. The caller ID indicated that the call was from outside the hotel.

"This is Zavier Jackson," Zavier answered in his 'I'm important at work' voice.

"Mr. Jackson, this is Siri Dawson from Channel Seven. I just wanted to thank you for your assistance this weekend," the smooth voice announced.

Zavier wondered if it was standard for reporters to call back random people who offered minimal information or assistance to "thank them". It suddenly clicked in Zavier's head that this fine man may be coming on to him.

"It was my pleasure, Mr. Dawson. It was an honor to meet you in person. Maybe we can have drinks or grab a bite to eat one day." Zavier was immediately embarrassed by his boldness. He had not dated or flirted with anyone in years and was surprised himself that he was so intrigued by this man.

"Please call me Siri, and I would love to get together with you. As a matter of fact, what do you have planned for dinner this evening?" Siri asked casually.

"Well, I don't really have any plans. What do you have in mind?" Zavier asked trying to mask his excitement.

"Let's meet at Einstein's on Juniper for dinner," Siri suggested.

"Sure thing. Let's say six?" Zavier responded.

"Sounds good. Looking forward to seeing you again," Siri said.

Zavier placed the phone on the receiver and just sat smiling for a few moments. He had not felt this kind of excitement for a long time. He was reluctant to give in completely to his euphoria for fear that he had misinterpreted Siri's intentions. What if Siri were straight and simply reaching out for male friendship? Although Zavier was obviously older, Siri could just be interested in establishing good heterosexual relationships with other seemingly professional men. Whatever the intent, Zavier felt good about the prospect of this new person in his life.

Zavier and Siri hit it off well and the conversation over dinner was very fluent and comfortable. Zavier found himself laughing more than he had in a long time. Only Calvin could make him laugh the way this gorgeous man did. The awkwardness he usually felt with men was nowhere to be found with Siri. Being with Siri was like being with someone he had known forever. This experience was a refreshing change from the lackadaisical evenings he endured on the few dates he had attempted over the past months. Zavier was pleasantly surprised at the wisdom and maturity of Siri after finding out that he was a full seven years younger than Zavier. Then he remembered that he himself had been eight years younger than Calvin.

The two attractive, professional men sat in the booth at the Midtown Atlanta restaurant for over an hour after they had finished the good meal. It was obvious that neither wanted to end the stimulating conversation that had run the spectrum from politics to religion. The gentlemen found that they shared similar, if not identical, views on every subject.

"I know we've already paid the check, but now I feel like having some dessert," Siri said looking around for the flirtatious gay server.

As he looked around, he noticed that several patrons in booths around them where looking in his direction, especially women and the few gay men who were dining there that night.

Zavier also noticed the attention they were getting and came up with a plan.

"I guess you're being recognized a lot more than you thought these days. Now I feel a little like we're on display. I have an idea. It's still early, so if you want to follow me home, I have a Sara Lee Cheesecake and we could continue our conversation there," Zavier said, again wondering if he was going too far; there still had been no real determining sign of whether this was a friendly dinner or a date.

"Ooh, I love Sara Lee Cheesecake. Let's go," Siri responded without hesitation.

Zavier was relieved that his suggestion did not seem to make Siri uncomfortable or suspicious at all. They quickly exited the restaurant and fortunately Siri had parked his shining clean red sports car on the same side street as Zavier.

Once they reached Zavier's beautiful mini-mansion, Zavier remotely opened the wide three-car garage exposing a Mercedes SUV, Calvin's white BMW which he refused to part with, and an open spot for the small Toyota that he drove everyday. The garage door closed as quickly as it had opened to receive its occupant, and within minutes, the frosted glass front door leading into the large foyer opened.

"Is this for real? Man, this place is unbelievable. And I saw those cars in the garage. You live here alone? What kind of money are you making at that hotel?" Siri asked in awe, stretching his neck to look around as if he were at a museum.

"I inherited this place and a pretty profitable stock in a very successful event planning business," Zavier explained.

"You're into event planning too?" Siri asked.

"Oh no. A lady who knows what she is doing runs the business. I just get a check every quarter and sign some papers from time to time when big decisions need two signatures. Taniesha, the woman who runs the business, has forty-nine percent ownership, so she rarely needs my input," Zavier answered.

"Wow, I felt a little strange letting you pick up the tab tonight. But who knew you were rich? Why do you work?" Siri joked.

"I'm not rich. Because of someone else's hard work, I am comfortable. I would not enjoy sitting around not working every day. But I must admit, it does feel good to know that if things went wrong for me at work, I would be o.k. I have someone very special to thank forever for making sure that I live well even after he is gone," Zavier responded as he lead the way to the living room, offering Siri a seat on the large sofa. At that moment it saddened him to think that David did not honor Darnell for this same gift.

"Is that Calvin Sharpe?" Siri asked, noticing a large portrait of Calvin hanging over the mantle. In the portrait, Calvin looked as regal and dignified as a prince. He wore a black tuxedo jacket and royal blue bowtie. He had a serious, wise expression on his face. His beautiful hazel eyes were liquid and full of love.

"Yes it is. As new as you are at Channel Seven, I'm surprised you recognize him. Calvin was my partner..." Zavier began slowly, not sure how Siri would take this first mention of his sexuality.

"Sharpe Enterprises! That's the event planning business. Oh, I'm so stupid. I get it now. This was Calvin Sharpe's house. And you were his..." Siri stumbled looking for the word.

"I was his partner, his lover." Zavier rescued Siri from this awkward place.

Siri told Zavier how he was the fact finder who had spoken to Calvin the same night he was killed and how he had hoped to be mentored by Calvin. Zavier was moved as Siri spoke of how much he respected Calvin's work and honored him as a real modern day hero.

"I did not get the opportunity to meet Mr. Sharpe in person but when he died, it hurt me more than I ever would have imagined. I remember feeling so empty and disappointed that the relationship we may have had would never be," Siri said in somber reflection.

Although Zavier was usually very slow to connect with guys, there was something very special about this man. Whether it was his refreshing intelligence, comfortable conversation, gorgeous appearance, or his apparent reverence for Calvin, Zavier knew he wanted to spend much more time with him.

Zavier and Siri talked until the wee hours of the morning, ending the evening with simple platonic pleasantries about how nice their conversation was. Nervousness set in on Zavier as he debated whether to shake Siri's hand as he left or give him a hug. He definitely wanted the hug, he inwardly was dying to feel that muscular chest that was so obviously taunting him through Siri's button down white shirt. He longed to stand against Siri, embraced in a hug and know that his crotch was touching Siri's. As he reached the door, his boldness betrayed him and he extended his hand and Siri responded by grabbing it and giving him a slight handshake. Siri held on to Zavier's hand far longer than a normal handshake should last and began to speak as he held it.

"You know Zavier, I haven't had such a good time with anyone in a long time. I really hope we can get together again very soon," Siri said, looking straight into Zavier's eyes as he spoke.

"I had a really good time too. I look forward to spending a lot more time with you in the future, if that's o.k. with you," Zavier said, realizing that Siri still held his hand.

"That's more than o.k.," Siri responded in a soft tone, pronouncing each word with syncopated emphasis.

At that moment, Zavier felt the force of Siri pulling him closer by the hand he yet held. When his body was within a couple of inches of Siri's, and he stood facing him so closely that he could feel Siri's warm breath, Siri tilted and lowered his head, closed his eyes, and allowed his full lips to find Zavier's. Zavier closed his eyes and felt small flashes of lightning shooting through his body as Siri's warm tongue snaked its way into Zavier's mouth. Zavier could feel his dick stiffen in his pants and as Siri pressed against him, he could feel Siri's apparently large package throbbing against him, but Zavier was not longing to have sex with Siri. He simply wanted to live the rest of his life in this kiss. The kiss became more and more passionate, but neither man removed his clothes. When Siri finally released Zavier from his spell, both men were wet from persperation.

"Oh my God! It's three a.m. We must have kissed for an hour. That's crazy!" Zavier exclaimed laughing slightly.

"Yeah, I've got to get to bed. But it was worth every minute," Siri said with a sneaky smile on his face.

Zavier and Siri saw more and more of each other from that night on. One night in April, just three months after meeting, Zavier and Siri had spent the evening at Siri's small Midtown condo watching the latest TV fad, reality TV, and subsequently found themselves cuddled up on Siri's soft black leather sofa. Neither Zavier nor Siri had spoken since the last commercial when the show ended and a new set of commercials ensued. Out of nowhere, Siri made a statement that blew Zavier's mind.

"Zavier, I think you know this, but... I... love you." Siri stumbled on the last three words.

Zavier, who was being held by Siri with his back to him, flipped over in Siri's arms and looked him in the eyes. This was the first time either of them had said these words to each other.

"Oh Siri, I love you too. I don't really know when I started loving you. It may have been love at first sight because I can't remember not loving you, but I do... I love you," Zavier said as the words came tumbling out of his mouth.

"Just be patient with me. This is hard for me. I have never been in love with a man before. I had a girlfriend in college and I think I loved her, but I never even knew it was possible to love another man like this until I got out of school and met friends in this lifestyle. I've only been with one other guy, and that was more of an experiment," Siri confessed.

"I understand Siri. I haven't always known how to be comfortable with loving another guy either. I thought I was in love a few times but found out that I really had only been in love once," Zavier said.

"With Calvin?" Siri asked.

"Yes, with Calvin. And now, with you. I honestly thought I could never love anyone again after I lost Calvin. But there is something about you that has touched my heart in a way that only Calvin had before. I find myself fascinated with you. I think about you all the time. I want to know everything there is to know about you. Calvin and I were together for five years and I never could get him to tell me anything about his childhood or family. I don't want to go through that again. I want to know your family. I want to know how you grew up. Everything," Zavier said with a sudden burst of energy.

"I will tell you everything and in time, you will know me better than anyone. But let me warn you, there's not much to it. My mother died in childbirth, so I grew up in my great aunt's home on the West End. My three older cousins are like siblings to me. They were all grown and out of the house by the time I became a teenager so I somewhat grew up alone. That's about it," Siri said, hunching his shoulders to indicate that he did not know what else to tell.

"Does your family know about your sexuality?" Zavier inquired genuinely interested in knowing all he could about the new love in his life.

"No. I know my aunt, who I call Nana because my cousins call her that, would probably be o.k. with it after the initial shock. However, my cousins are a different story. I am just not ready to deal with that right now," Siri answered.

"So I guess I won't be meeting the family," Zavier said disappointed that he may be in another relationship with someone with whom he could have no interaction with his family.

Siri immediately recognized the disappointment in Zavier's expression.

"You know what? Nana always wants me to come over for Sunday dinner. Why don't you go with me this Sunday? This time, I'll introduce you as a friend if you're o.k. with that. It will just be us and Nana, who is the sweetest lady I know," Siri offered.

"Sure. That sounds great. At this point, I guess we are just friends anyway," Zavier said.

"No, I'm sure we're a lot more than friends," Siri said and began to passionately kiss Zavier.

"My goodness Siri. Your friends are just as handsome as you are. Come on Zavier, give Nana a hug too," Nana said as she pulled Zavier into her soft bosom patting him violently on his back.

Zavier had found himself surprisingly nervous as he and Siri arrived at the modest white bungalow in the revitalizing West End community of Atlanta. The small yard was meticulously landscaped with blooming bushes and a clean rock garden near the porch. Zavier found it hard to believe that Siri, for all his sophistication, came from such a simple and homely beginning. Before they had reached the porch, Nana swung the screen door wide open beckoning Siri to rush into her tight, loving embrace.

Zavier's nerves were settled after meeting Nana and seeing for himself that she indeed may be the sweetest lady alive. She held both men's hands as they entered the cluttered but clean home. The delicious odor of a cooling peach cobbler dominated the house and Zavier's appetite began to leap for joy as Nana swept Siri and Zavier directly to the dinner table, which had been set with baked chicken, cornbread dressing, homemade macaroni and cheese, collard greens, sweet potatoes, and homemade rolls.

After Nana had stuffed the two men to the point of misery, they left the table and retired to the small living room. The room was eclectically decorated with collectibles, inexpensive antiques, and old framed photos.

"Nana, that meal was unbelievable. I haven't had a meal like that since I left South Georgia twenty years ago," Zavier complimented, taking the liberty of affectionately calling her Nana.

"Oh baby, that's no Georgia cooking. That's Mississippi cooking there," Nana boasted.

"You're from Mississippi? My...best friend was from Mississippi," Zavier said, careful not to make Siri or Nana uncomfortable by referring to Calvin as his partner.

"Really? What part of Mississippi is he from?" Nana inquired.

Zavier felt himself building an even greater bond with Nana through this distant connection. He knew that two sure ways to bring joy to senior citizens were showing interest in their memories and relating to their heritage. And Mississippi was apparently Nana's heritage.

"I can never remember the name of the little town. It was an animal's name, like fox or horse. Something like that." Zavier struggled to remember the name.

"Oh, Mississippi is full of little one stop towns with names like that. I grew up in a little place named Woolfe," Nana said with a chuckle.

"Woolfe! That's it. Woolfe. My friend was from Woolfe, Mississippi," Zavier declared, excited at the coincidence.

"No baby, he probably isn't from Woolfe. Woolfe isn't half the size of the West End. If he is from there then I'm sure I know his family. What's his name?" Nana inquired smiling at the prospect of meeting someone else from Woolfe. In the fifty-plus years she had been in Atlanta, she had never run across anyone else from Woolfe living there.

"He passed away a couple of years ago, but his name was Calvin Sharpe," Zavier said as he noticed an eight by ten photo of a pubescent Siri wearing a neat blue pinstriped suit and bright gold tie holding a trophy about half his size and standing under a banner reading "Georgia State Spelling Bee".

The smile disappeared from Nana's face as she seemed to gravely consider Zavier's statement. Without a word, she rose, went to her bedroom, and returned carrying an old, beat up brown shoebox; the kind made wide enough for boots. Siri moved closer to her on the velvet-like upholstered sofa.

"Nana, what's wrong? What's in that box?" Siri asked. He knew it was not like Nana to grow all of a sudden quiet.

"You know boys, they say that what you don't know can't hurt you. Well sometimes, what you don't know *can* hurt you." Nana stopped and gazed into Siri's beautiful hazel eyes before continuing.

Nana removed the flimsy lid from the tattered shoebox and laid it carefully on the coffee table. She then took a stack of letters and old photos out of the box and laid them beside the lid. At the bottom of the box was a paperback green book. Nana slowly, dramatically handed the thick book to Siri who accepted it with curiosity.

He examined the cover, which read, *Swahili to English Translation Dictionary*. He took the book, handling it as if it were nitroglycerin and subject to explode at any moment. The book was filled with Swahili words in alphabetical order translated to their English equivalents. Page three-forty-one was marked with a red ribbon. Circled with a red pen was the word that captured Siri's attention and, to his surprise, caused a tear to trickle from the corner of his eye: *"Siri: (noun) A great secret."*

Tucked tightly in the crease of the book on that page was a white envelope, now yellowing with the stain of age. Siri took the fragile envelope from its longtime resting place, gently prying it loose as it was stuck to the page. It was not addressed but was stuffed with a sheet of wide ruled tablet paper. The fraying edges from where the sheet had been torn out of the tablet had been meticulously pulled off. Siri carefully unfolded the letter; the creases of the folds were aged and worn enough to cause the letter to fall apart if it wasn't handled gently. Realizing Zavier's curiosity, Siri read the letter aloud.

October 4, 1980

Dear Calvin,

I am writing this letter to you because I think it is only right for you to know what is happening, but I don't think I will mail it. So I don't really know why I'm writing it. I guess it just makes me feel better.

Calvin, I am so sad right now and there is no one I can talk to. You are the only one I could really be myself with and tell my real secrets to and now I don't even have you. I want to come home and be with you.

I know you think I left you and I don't care about you but you just don't understand. Calvin, back in February I started feeling sick everyday. I was so scared I had cancer like my mama had died from. My daddy took me to the doctor and we found out I was not sick but I was pregnant. Calvin, I was pregnant with your child.

My daddy went to talk to your grandmother about it and she told him that she didn't want your future to be messed up because of no baby. And she told him that he had to make me leave and have the baby and give it away or I couldn't come back home. She said we couldn't tell nobody, not even you. She told him if he didn't do what she said, she would tell everybody not to give him no work. She said she would make sure nobody believed it was your baby anyway and you know how everybody be listening to Miss Letha to do what she say. So I'm going to leave this pretty little boy here in Atlanta with my Aunt so she can raise him and give him a good home and all the love me and you never got. It will be good for him to grow up in the city anyway so he can have a real future and not have to fight so hard for it like us in the country.

Calvin, you ought to see this little boy, he just a tiny baby but he look just like you already. But he got just enough of me in him to not look as white as you do. His hair is brown just like yours and he got them light brown pretty eyes and pink lips. It is killing me that I'm going to have to leave him here. I don't want him to think I didn't love him so I made my aunt promise she's going to tell him that I died. Really, I will die a little when I have to leave this baby here. I hope that one day when all this is past us, you will get to meet this son of yours. You are so smart and such a special person, I know you would be a good role model for him.

I am not sad that I had this baby, I love him. Thank you for giving him to me if only for this little time I get to spend with him.

Love,
Zelda

P.S. I finally found a good use for that Swahili book you bought me at the library book sale.

***

About the Author

Glen Collins attended the University of Memphis in the early '90s, and while his official major was Management Information Systems, he enjoyed writing throughout his college career. Glen moved to Kansas City, Missouri where he owned and operated a small printing business, publishing small projects for local businesses and artists. Today Glen resides in Atlanta, Georgia and is working on his next novel.

Email Glen at glencollinswriter@yahoo.com.

Printed in the United States
144153LV00003BA/9/P

9 781438 961415